To Liza.
Thanks so much
for all your encouragement
and support!
& with you
    good wine
    good drama
        good life!

S.A.

GOD AWFUL THIEF

Acevedo

S. ACEVEDO

THREE
POINTS
PUBLISHING

The text type was set in Adobe Caslon

ISBN 978-0-9863207-3-6 (hardcover)
ISBN 978-0-9863207-4-3 (eBook)

First Edition
Printed in the United States of America
15 16 17 18 19 — 6 5 4 3 2 1

For Valerie and Keith,
whose boundless creativity and insight
get me further – and farther – every day.

CONTENTS

Chapter 1

CURTAINS UP

The hypocritical snobs in Olympus frown at my love of grape. But let it be known: if it weren't for my drinking, the mortal and immortal worlds alike would have been taken over by a swindler who can con sober minds. So let us all praise wine!

Pondering it later, I wondered if maybe I shouldn't have let the takeover happen. Either option, a rebellion or a furious fight for the status quo, would be fun – and extremely dramatic. Gods, I love drama. Still, I don't like someone poking around in my head, so interference became my best revenge.

Act I. Scene 1.

(Setting: The supposedly hollow cavity between my ears – or, the once vibrant chamber now rotted by sloshing wine – depending on whom you ask. As the god of wine and theatre, I often dream of stagehands dressed in Olympic laurels. Tonight's dream, however, is interrupted by a shadowy figure

nudging into the recesses of my memory. This may be shown as a figure in black entering stage right and slithering his way around sparse, broken down furniture.)

"Mmmm," thinks my Sleep Self to the unwelcome intruder. "Who are you?"

The figure lifts its cowled head. I see a pale countenance dominated by a large, downturned nose, like a parrot's beak, and guarded, olive-green eyes. I know the face.

"Tell me your secrets," it speaks.

"No," is my answer.

"Tell me," it demands.

"Go screw yourself." Or something like that. Wine does dull the memory.

The dream dissolves and reforms itself into a bedroom scene. **(Stagehands, be clever. Drape cloth over the furniture to suggest a bed.)**

I see the figure lurking over Jupiter's inclined form. The King of the Gods mumbles answers to every question.

The scene swirls until it finds itself in murky depths. The same shadowy figure floats above Neptune's watery berth. **(Stagehands, cue the stage wiring.)** The Water Lord hums the secrets of his soul, bubbles rising with each breath.

I understood then what was happening and wonder if you do, too. Don't fret if you're as in the dark as

Neptune's domain. The drama is set to unfold. I made my choice, the option most likely to create conflict. Delicious conflict. The savory filling of the best stories.

I'd not let Mercury succeed, that greedy, two-faced delver in dreams. The god of commerce, theft, and the unconscious may *think* he can swindle, steal, and connive his way to the top, but wine and love *do* go together. I sided with Cupid if for no other reason than to foul the plans of the god who disrupted my dreams.

Chapter 2

THE WATER BOILS

Cupid, the newly reinstated god of love, zigzagged above a raging sea. Even his new, power-infused, blue-tipped wings – an upgrade given by Jupiter for saving the kingdom – barely got him past the huge waves leaping skyward from the wind-whipped sea below.

Only a few quiet weeks had passed since Cupid regained his crown, though his misadventure remained fresh in his mind and vivid nightmares continued to contaminate his confidence. Fighting The Lord of the Dead and battling his beasts has a way of sticking with you. Even so, Cupid tried to forget such unpleasantries. He most uncharacteristically distanced himself from the limelight, which isn't easy to do when you believe that the world needs love, and that you yourself are lovely, and that everything's made better with you around it. For the sake of restoring normalcy to the kingdom, Mr. Love himself tried to keep his head down, do his work, and steer clear of controversy. Yet here he was again dodging trouble.

Cupid flew erratically, flapped furiously. His long, brown, curly hair whipped his face, leaving flushed welts across the white plain. His pooch of a belly jiggled as he struggled to clear the tempestuous, watery upsurges. All the while, he racked his brain to understand what he could have possibly done to anger his great uncle, the sea god. Those salt water hooks would drag him down and drown him given the chance.

Even with distance and speed, Cupid knew he wasn't going to outmaneuver the raging waters for long. He spotted an island ahead, mountainous and lush with vegetation. *Not exactly a safe port*, Cupid thought, keenly aware of Neptune's ability to create earthquakes powerful enough to split that spit of land in half.

But I can't stay out in the open much longer, he thought. *I'll take my chances.*

Lowering the tips of his magnificent wings, Cupid soared upward. When he felt slightly safer, somewhat more out of reach of the giant, briny waves, he rocketed horizontally toward the oasis. The water below him seethed. Tall, teal blue curls rolled in pursuit.

Cupid peered more closely into the froth and saw a merman, porpoising face-up just below the surface. The bearded manfish was staring hard. When their eyes met, the fish-guy raised a pink conch to his lips and blew.

Cupid heard nothing but knew in a heartbeat who that aquatic being was: not his great uncle the sea god, no. Neptune looked nothing like this feral merman. Besides, Neptune's method of stirring waves was by circling his golden trident or commanding his powerful horses to gallop or maybe even just thinking about it. But Neptune's *son* Triton did it by blowing into a conch shell. Even underwater.

In the time it took Cupid to understand, a giant water-hand shot up and swatted. It grazed his feet, and Cupid tumbled mid-air. He saw hundreds of fish being tossed around inside it – as if they deserved the mistreatment any more than he. Cupid regained his balance just as the fist threatened to pummel him again.

The god of love was being loved by no one now.

Cupid decided he didn't much like this game, if it was a game, which it probably was because *everyone* loved him. So he pumped his wings hard. As he outpaced the fishy fist, his strength surprised him; it had been some time since he'd flown in earnest. Then again, he reminded himself, he *was* a god, and a marvelous one at that.

As Cupid breached the imaginary plane separating land from sea, he spun to see what the water appendage would do. Surprisingly, it stopped its forward progress and collapsed like rain.

Panting, Cupid raised his own hand to halt the water droplets. He could control water in various ways: he could float on a single molecule and gather huge balls of it from the air at will. But this particular water refused to obey. It didn't halt mid-air like he wanted. Instead, it kept falling and plopped into the surf rolling onto the beach. The water had ended its pursuit – but not its animosity.

Salt water, he thought. *Different than fresh water. But I've moved salt water before, in the Roman Colosseum.*

Huh. Had Neptune allowed *it back then?*

Shifting his focus beyond the now harmless surf lapping the sandy beach, Cupid watched Triton rise above the water's skin.

Triton's heavily muscled torso heaved on each breath. His shoulders were barnacled with shells pouring water from within. He rose to the ends of his long, double-fluked tail while the rest of the snake-like appendage writhed and curled. That sight of mastery was one every sailor feared:

> *"E'er Triton stands atop his tail,*
> *ships anon be sunk by gale."*

Cupid got the distinct impression that the sea's messenger god was sending *him* the same message.

Cupid gently flapped his wings, backing into the palms. Once he'd disappeared in the greenery, he allowed himself a moment to think, drifting well above the forest floor, lost in thought.

Just weeks ago he'd fought Pluto, The God of the Underworld, and the evil mastermind's minion, planted specifically to overthrow Olympus. *Posers,* Cupid thought.

Despite his dismissive attitude toward it now, The Love God suffered a great deal of indignity at losing a duel to Pluto's servant – and then having to regain the trust of his grandfather, Jupiter, to save the kingdom. At the time, it seemed that his Uncle Neptune had helped Cupid in the fight, so why was Neptune's son now trying to drown him?

Why would anyone want to harm me? Cupid asked himself. *I'm the god of love, the maharajah of pleasure, and the most beautiful sight in Olympus. Well, Tamara's great eye candy, too, as any girl with me should be. And wait a minute – no one could even be mad about* her, *either, because* me *lavishing my many affections and bedroom skills on* her *means I'm not lavishing them on* their *women. Even if their women still secretly want it.*

(It seems that near banishment from the kingdom was not quite enough to slay Cupid's ego. But the braggart was bragging slightly less often. It was a start.)

Shaking off the idea of unrequited love and jealous lovers, Cupid returned to thoughts of his immediate situation. He could fly high enough to avoid even the loftiest waves, he knew, but he wanted to understand what prompted the need. Clearly Triton was in no mood for a calm, god-to-god discussion.

What's Triton's problem? he wondered.

Cupid looked down at his clothes and sighed. They were soaked, his grey suit darkened nearly black. The ultra modern Spanish Grey hue was a new look for him, from the day he and Tamara had officially paired up and he'd ditched his sparkly white suit. The fashion change signified a more serious and committed life, a shot across the bow against his own haughty hubris. Put simply, he intended to show less flash.

Problem was, his new duds were staid, and he missed the bling. *Maybe I'll add rhinestones,* he mused. *Or ruffles.* He ran his fingers along the lapels' sopping edges.

(And as he pondered, dear reader, imagine how I marveled. I saw all this through Cupid's eyes while I myself lay on my hammock in my forest home. Seeing life's events through another's eyes? The transformation is a voyeur's dream, and what is theatre if not voyeurism of the living condition?

It appeared logical to me that Mercury, in his nighttime traveling and rummaging through unconscious and unguarded minds, had failed to close this particular door. I unwittingly alighted upon Cupid's mind in my waking moments and could hear his every thought, loud as my own. Hearing him was as effortless as granting a foolish mortal his fondest wish. Say, have I ever told you the story of my bestowing The Midas Touch? It is a harsh lesson in avarice and a nearly tragic tale. But I digress. Back to Cupid's plight.)

The love lord, apparently uncomfortable in dripping attire, bunched the edges of his lapel in his hands and squeezed.

Now, be it told, *fresh* water might have left the merino wool willingly, without insult, but not *this* water, riled to anger by a salt water deity. The droplets held fast to the fabric and suddenly moved as one. The suit jerked left – with Cupid in it.

"Whoa!" he shouted. The suit halted and reversed course. "Whoa! Stop!" Cupid commanded. In answer, the suit pistoned left, right, and left again, shaking him like a maraca. Cupid flailed. His wings, arms, legs, everything moved, but none of it prevented his suit from pulling him wherever it wished – and it wished to haul him into the canopy of the nearest tree. Cupid was yanked upward and brushed by the soft rush of leaves before being stabbed by the tree's tangled branches.

Cupid's waterlogged suit changed direction and plunged downward, pulling him onto lower branches. The branches either immediately snapped or held strong, scraping Cupid as he passed them. Cupid finally collided against a lower, fatter bough and grabbed hold before sliding underneath. He held on and panted for breath.

The suit slammed to an angry halt. It swung side to side. It shook violently. Unable to continue its downward plunge, the suit changed tactic and threw itself back upward onto the bough before scraping Cupid along it like cheese on a grater.

"Stop! Stop!" Cupid bellowed as the brown-grey bark cut into his flesh and the wood's milky sap seeped into his cuts. Bits of skin-shredding bark scattered in every direction. Cupid looked up and saw that the tree's entire crown shook. Anyone watching would have thought a family of orangutans swung in hysterics. Bark rained into his eyes.

Cupid extended a hand blindly, hoping for any change of circumstance. He managed to wrench loose a handful of leaves from a connecting twig. Reaching out again, struggling, he felt something different, something fleshy, and grabbed hold.

A hiss told him he'd made a bad choice, and the notice was confirmed when teeth clamped down.

"Whaaaaaaah!" Cupid screamed. He opened his watering eyes and saw that he'd grabbed the fat hind legs and spiked tail of a long green iguana. The poor thing's puny front legs were scratching desperately to cling to its perch. Its neck curled back to bite its attacker. It wasn't going to be able to hold Cupid's weight a second longer. The affronted lizard whipped its tail in defense and slapped him, spikes up, hard across the face.

Howling in fresh pain, Cupid released him, but too late. The iguana lost its tenuous grip, dropped to the forest floor, and bounced.

Cupid knew he was next. As the suit pulled downward, ready to plunge him to the earth, the legendary lover demanded, "STOP!"

The suit halted just a fraction of a second, apparently obeying him or simply failing to acknowledge gravity.

Not wasting a moment, Cupid grabbed the suit lapels and wrested off the jacket. Its sleeves snagged Cupid's bow and quiver, which dropped to the forest floor. The falling arrows just missed the iguana **(which is good because who knows how a reptile in love might act?)**. The jacket shot off toward the sea and Triton, who was no doubt controlling it.

Maniac! thought Cupid.

But the maniac's assault wasn't over. Cupid's finely tailored trousers tipped him upside down and swung him to bash his royal head against the hardwood's trunk. **(Cupid's puffy hair made him look like a living drum mallet, the tree his instrument.)**

Cupid barked louder than a howler monkey. Without thinking **(because, really, it could have turned out ugly)**, Cupid tugged on his zipper and dropped out of his pants. His body plummeted toward the ground while his pants zoomed off toward the sea. Just before Cupid hit soil, his shirt, traditional diaper, and shoes, the only clothes remaining, flipped him face up and halted; Cupid's head whiplashed against the ground.

Our battered beloved groaned in pain. His neck was jarred, and his body only lacked a final slam onto Earth to finish him off. Cupid didn't want to see what his few remaining articles of clothing might have in mind, so he reached beneath him and felt through the forest undergrowth for his bow and quiver. Snagging an arrow, Cupid whipped it forward. He dragged the arrowhead across the front of his shirt, shearing it from neck to hip, and his diaper from hip to leg, all while pushing his shoes off his heels.

These clothes were a lot less wet than his outerwear – but still damp enough for a sea god to govern. They whisked away, dropping Cupid, naked as the day he was born, onto terra firma. I wondered if Cupid would ever get his diaper back. Then I doubted that he'd want to, seeing as he was going for reinvention.

Our charming nudist sputtered, the wind knocked out of him. He struggled to suck in air – but could not. I unfortunately felt his terror through our unusual but ter-rifically entertaining connection **(I could breathe just fine, thank you so much for asking.).** Cupid couldn't feel his lungs at all, but he could feel the mossy earth at his back and the nock of his bow digging into his shoulder blade and, finally, sharp nails climb up the back of his head.

Cupid, unable to move any other part of his body, rolled his eyes up toward the top of his head. I heard him worry that something was crawling through his beautiful hair, the precious brown curls that so many ladies dreamed of wrapping around their fingers.

What emerged through the split ends of the longest curl was the head of the bright green iguana. It crested the top of Cupid's forehead and looked down into his eyes, the same grey-green eyes that could make the world swoon. (So esteemed the narcissist.)

The lizard hissed and continued its scratchy, scaly walk over the god's face and chest. Cupid noticed broken spikes all along its back and knew he'd caused them. He couldn't feel much remorse; he was at the time trying to save himself. And he couldn't apologize even if he wanted, his breath still gone from his lungs. Instead Cupid watched as the creature approached his abs, scratched good and deep into his divine flesh, raised its tail, and left a parting gift of green goo before darting back to the cover of the forest. Bits of bark and leaves continued to rain down from the tree and stuck to the goo like jimmies on frosting.

Cupid felt his chest release, and he inhaled deeply. It triggered a coughing fit, but, once he again had control over his faculties, he lifted his heavy head and shoulders and propped himself on his elbows. He looked down at his naked, wounded body and noticed something even more distressing. He was swelling. And blistering. He raised a hand before his face and saw its cuts soaking up the tree's white sap like a sponge absorbs water.

This isn't normal, He thought.

Cupid looked up at the tree's trunk **(freshly chafed, thanks to him)** and saw a sign posted about five feet up:

> # BEWARE
> ## Manchineel tree
> ## Fruit, leaves, sap
> # POISONOUS!
> ### Do not eat, handle, or shelter
> ### under when raining.

I'm in trouble, Cupid thought **(waaaay later than I would have come to that conclusion)**. His eyes itched. His fingers felt fat and numb. Through his quickly clogging ears, he heard a rustling in the trees to his left **(It was actually a crashing through the trees, like a herd of charging bison.)**. He turned to feast his eyes and spotted a tree being felled by a giant pair of legs. Massive, knotty knees bent. A hand as wide across as he was tall came into view.

And before Cupid could understand, he was swinging upside down once again, this time high *above* the treetops. The hand that held him connected to a one-eyed giant. And the giant was licking its lips.

Chapter 3

AN EYE FOR DANGER

Cupid didn't know nearly as much about cyclopes as he should. He knew they're his second cousins, that is, the children of his great uncle Neptune. But, see, there's the problem. For the Love God, following his family tree was always a brain fry, and here's a perfect example why. The cyclopes are Neptune's kids. Neptune is the brother of Cupid's grandfather, Jupiter, who isn't really his grandfather, not by blood anyway, because Cupid's dad, Mars, wasn't begotten by Jupiter -- that is, he wasn't born from Jupiter [who is a prolific philanderer, by the way]. No, Mars was created by Cupid's biological grandmother, Juno [who's Jupiter's wife - and sister] when she touched a flower to her belly and pop! it made a baby. Then there's Cupid's mom, Venus, who was born after a bit of her father was thrown into the sea, so she didn't have any full siblings, either, just half-siblings. So you can see why, with all the intrigue in the family, Cupid has a hard time keeping up.

Besides the vague kinship, there are a few other things commonly known about cyclopes: They're man-eaters, brutally strong, and unyieldingly stubborn.)

If this thing plans to keep me, Cupid thought, *no family chat will change its mind.*

With that, Cupid raised his bloodied, rashy chest upward toward his feet. It was harder doing a hanging sit up than he cared to admit, although he told himself it was because he was being swung. (Suuuuuuure. If I can admit that my fondness for grape teeters toward the obscene, he should be able to admit that he's out of shape.)

Our Fantasy of Fitness, that Sovereign of Sit Ups, did, in fact, manage a full sit up. He wrapped his quickly swelling fingers around his ankles and pulled. Nothing. Not an inch.

The cyclops must have felt movement, though. It looked at its quarry and shook it violently. The world reeled. Cupid dropped again to dangling and was barely able to keep his lunch. (The feeling didn't upset me nearly as much as it did him. As you might imagine, I, the god of merrymaking, have long overcome the sense of queasiness that comes with the occasional loss of equilibrium. The ability to steady one's stomach is a skill. Back to upside-down Cupid.)

In a mere few strides, the giant holding him reached a clearing that was obviously used by more than just he. Six stone-encircled, earthen fire pits sat cold and black awaiting their next use. Cupid wondered for a moment when that next use would be. Strewn around the pits were hundreds of charred, blackened bones sporting deep gouges that looked ominously like teeth marks. There were long, straight bones that might have been femurs and curved, sun-bleached ones that looked like ribs.

Cupid gulped and thrashed to get free.

The cyclops lifted his catch and slapped Cupid onto the ground like a dead fish, again knocking the breath out of him. Cupid even looked a bit like a fish, naked and gasping for breath.

The giant then tossed beside him a great, charred log with thick ropes wound around the ends just the right distance apart to bind Cupid's hands and feet. Our captive no longer wondered when the next meal would be; he knew it'd be however long it took his cousin to roast him on a spit.

(By now, I'm fully awake. Cupid's confusion during Triton's chase was the thing that initially stirred me from my slumber. Then his torture against the poisonous tree forced me from my bed to find my own relief in liquid analgesic. But now I must finally act. Stirring a pot reduces the bubble in the boiling, and I'm not one to calm a boil, but I have no desire to feel his bones crunch and his muscles tear as a monster makes a meal of him, my mental magnet. So, fine. If I must leave the comfort of my own home, where's my flask?

Anyway, dear reader, by the time I got myself together and readied my chariot and drove it over the same waters that attacked Cupid, our roped Romeo was in seriously bad straits. He was tightly bound to the log and propped against another manchineel tree. Cupid flexed his back to keep his startlingly white butt from touching the blistering bark again. He wheezed. His eyes distended.

Still, he must have been able to hear because he turned his face toward me when my chariot glided to a halt next to the fire pit which was destined to be his final resting place. Well, I suppose his final resting place would be inside the cyclop's belly, but, lo and behold, the one-eyed creature was nowhere in sight.)

Cupid's brow rose. He was quite surprised to see me, although I imagine that he could only barely see me.

Who's that?! Cupid's question rang in my head. He squinted through his temporary blindness, and I laughed at his assessment: *Youngish guy. Skinny. In a ... silver, maybe, chariot driven by ... black panthers? Oh, it's Bacchus,* he thought, and then rather uncharitably summed me up as androgynous.

(I'd hardly call myself androgynous; I just don't go for massive, bulging muscles and all the work involved in maintaining them. I'd rather spend my time socializing and perfecting the art of blending spirits for merrymaking. In fact, plenty of times, my work makes his work easier. Never mind. Back to our bound beloved.)

"Hello, Cupid!" I hailed. "I saw the trouble with Triton ... and the rest. Where's your cousin, the cyclops?"

Cupid puzzled in his head a moment as to how I'd have seen his morning, but I heard his thoughts as he decided that the gods have plenty of ways to see the goings-on around them. He also hoped his misadventures weren't going to be the source of renewed gossip.

"He's, uh, gone, I guess, to look for firewood,

probably."

"You, sir, are in quite a pickle," I teased, stepping out of my chariot and adjusting my wreath of ivy leaves. I'm very fond of my modest, biologically sensitive head wear as it makes all the other gods' fancy-dancy, bejeweled crowns look as pretentious as their wearers.

I whispered to my panthers to lie low. The three of them stalked into the forest, pulling my chariot along. The ivy leaves engraved along the chariot's edges rippled as if to say goodbye.

"Um, yeah," Cupid answered simply. "A pickle."

(I liked that about him. He's not all puffed up in himself. Well, yeah, sure he is. They all are, but at least he's not going to pass off some phony baloney about his *wanting* to end up the way he was, like he'd planned it that way. Just one look at him would tell anyone that no one planned that.)

"You probably should get yourself out of it," I advised simply. I felt that that encouragement basically solved the problem. Cupid was a god and could figure it out his own way, and I really did have to search a bit for grape vine. I waved toward my departing chariot, and my thyrsus zoomed out of it and into my hand. I heard Cupid's thoughts in which he recognized my "pine-coney divining rod." He's basically right. He'd fix his problem, and I'd fix mine.

"Wait," demanded Cupid. "You came here, all this

way, to tell me to help myself? I could have done that without you." He tried to blink his huge eyes in incredulity, but all that happened was a strange quiver within the engorged lids.

"And I'm sure you will. I just wanted to see it for myself (-*and get involved only if I absolutely must to avoid feeling your pain*, I thought.). You being such a *powerful* god, I wanted to watch the action in person."

Cupid huffed, and I stepped out of the clearing and into the forest. I held out my thyrsus. The pine-cone head led the rod to swivel right. I held out my hand in that direction, and a wild grape vine shot into it. Easy peasy. Then I turned and walked back toward Cupid.

I was an ally, basically on his side, but I had to make sure he could handle himself before I fully committed. I talked, told him some of my theatre stories and about my strange dream last night, while he struggled, first to call up water, which wouldn't obey him, then to call his arrows. Those did obey as much as they could and shot toward him, presumably to cut the ropes. But they could only get within a few meters before being halted by an invisible force. They'd shake and try other angles but ultimately fail to reach their master. Eventually, they all splintered trying.

"Triton's setting up a water vapor wall, or maybe Neptune's controlling the salt water that splashed onto them," I offered helpfully.

Cupid didn't think it was helpful. I heard him think, *Ogler.*

I couldn't deny the accusation and so I laughed and leaned against the next nearest tree – not a manchineel; I checked first.

Cupid positively couldn't squirm his way free, as his swelling limbs had tightened the ropes to the point of cutting flesh. I watched him settle into silence and think. Finally, I felt the air change. It sweetened with the unmistakable scent of wine and cheese and walnuts and dark chocolate. All my favorite things. *Ah,* I thought. *He's pushing Peace and Goodwill, his own musky form of "get along." I wonder why.*

Through the brush, I heard rustling. Then crashing. Then pounding. And a second later, the cyclops who'd put Cupid into this mess bounded into the clearing with an armful of firewood, enough to build a cabin. (*It must wash up onshore,* I thought idly, *by Neptune's hand, because felling that much wood for one simple meal would wipe out the island's forest in a week.*) I stepped behind my tree to watch the events unfold.

Cupid huffed again and kept pushing P&G. To my seeing, it was having no affect on Mr. Big Eye. The behemoth just kept building its fire and probably imagining Cupid as a meaty marshmallow ready for the roasting.

While the giant stoked the fire and Cupid fought in his own way, I grew bored. It took a long time for me to understand why Cupid resorted to P&G. A. Long. Time. As long as it takes island snails to crawl out from the rocks and wood under which they shelter, as long as it takes them to squirm their way over to him, as long as it takes for them to squiggle up to the ropes binding hands and feet, and as long as it takes for them to slime-ify his extremities enough to slip free. (Truth be told, I missed most of it. After seeing the snails appear, I slid down onto my haunches, enjoyed my grape, and may have fallen back asleep. Eventually, I startled at hearing a new fire crackling to life and looked over just in time to see Cupid slip his hands free of the top ropes and bring them down to help loosen the ankle ropes. The giant was loping his way over.)

"Better hurry, Snail God!" I called quietly. "Here comes the chef!" I was going to make a joke about escargot but didn't fancy being heard by the cuisinier.

The giant roared in rage when his eye saw his prey half free. He lunged forward and swiped a mammoth hand.

Cupid ducked as the beefy mitt grabbed hold of the log and lifted. Before he was tugged along, Cupid slid his ankles free, simultaneously freeing a few snails from their entwinement and sending them cascading through the air toward their burrows below. He leapt aloft and reached the cyclops' eye before the goliath even noticed he'd lost his meal.

Cupid paused a moment, and I heard in my head his deep desire to taunt the giant before leaving, but his swollen eyes couldn't see more than a giant beige blob, and thus he didn't dare risk being recaptured. Cupid beat his wings hard and was away before his kin swiped.

(I stayed hunched behind my tree, watching the enraged cyclops howl incoherently and hurl skyward every bit of firewood that wasn't ablaze. Then the beast gave chase through the woods, too dim-witted to realize his confinement to land hindered catching anything that flew. Once he was well distanced from the clearing, I stepped back into it and called my panthers.

I was pleased with Cupid's ingenuity and decided that, yes, I'd keep helping him. *This is fun*, I decided. And – rather generously, I thought – I'd even help him get back home.)

Chapter 4

CORNERED

Cupid flew nearly all the way back to Olympus before he decided to stop outside The Mist surrounding the heavenly gates and duck into a cumulus cloud.

I caught up in my chariot and hovered just outside the watery mass to peer in. Cupid was furiously grabbing bits of cloud to form makeshift shorts. You'd think that a god who could normally manipulate water very well would be better able to more evenly spread its vapor; it's no different than spreading wet cement, and even mortals can do that.

I heard him curse me in his head, thinking me at best unhelpful and at worst a pervert. So says Mr. Love himself. I didn't get mad, though; Cupid didn't know how much I'd helped him already.

"I say!" I shouted, laying on my British accent thick enough to please Shakespeare himself. "See'st thou this sweet sight? How came these things to pass?"

"Cut it out!" hollered Cupid, not at all appreciating The Bard as much as a god should.

"As you like it," I retorted. "I assume you'd rather fly back yourself then – in your cloud shorts over Paradise Plaza at high noon. It'll be lunchtime, Cupid. You'll have a very fine audience for your nearly naked cameo. My, whatsoever will the critics say?"

Cupid stopped spreading vapor over his pudgy belly button and glared my way – well, as much as someone with swollen eyelids can glare.

"O-o-o-o-o-r," I offered, "you could hop into my chariot, tuck yourself down, and I'll take you quietly and securely to your castle. I've been wanting to meet your lovely new lady, and I'm sure she'll appreciate me backing up your story, seeing as how you'll be arriving home au naturel."

Cupid thrust out his hand while maintaining his glare. I held his eyes, too. It's far easier for a drunk than anyone brutally sober to hold an uncomfortable stare. After about thirty seconds (I knew he'd cave.), he lowered his eyes to catch his bow and quiver which had traveled a long way at his summons. Once he'd slung them over his shoulder and patted on a bit more protective vapor, he drifted my way.

What is Bacchus up to? he asked himself, and I chuckled at hearing the question in my own head. I'd explain it to him for the second time back at his place.

The panthers snarled. Cupid stepped into my chariot with seeming unconcern, but I heard his thoughts, and he was worried that their leather reins might snap.

I dreamed up many uncivilized taunts in the few moments that it took him to settle down deep into my chariot, but I held my tongue. (Only the inexperienced share their every thought.) After a few minutes, we landed with loud panther roars on the generous, rose-framed front lawn of Cupid Castle. (My cats like to announce our presence; it gives our hosts time to properly feed and water us during the visit.)

Cupid hopped out of the chariot and stomped toward his front door. I assumed the unspoken invitation had been given, and I followed. When he reached it, he ducked in and nearly slammed the lovely silver-lined portal in my face, but I had the presence of mind to dodge in first.

Nuts, I heard him think.

"It's all right, Cupid. Nothing damaged. Thanks for your concern."

Cupid's lips thinned as he held back commentary that I nonetheless heard. *The least he could do is stay off my lawn.*

"Park in back, please," I called over my shoulder, and my panthers shouldered ahead, pulling the buggy. I was sure that, once they reached the side of the castle, they'd shake loose the reins for their customary prowl of new territory.

Turning back, I decided to satisfy my curiosity about his abode and find something more favorable to look at than he. I found it in an instant. Across the vast, white-walled vestibule, walking barefoot from the Great Room, approached the most enchanting vision I'd seen in a long, long time.

A marvelously graceful and warmly smiling young woman hesitated not a moment to approach, plant a kiss on my unjustifiably lucky companion, and place a welcoming hand on my shoulder to invite me in. She was so unconcerned as to who I might be, so very ready to open her home to me, that I was momentarily shocked. Such unquestioning hospitality is a lost art even among the gods, and this lovely creature surely did not glow as an immortal goddess would. Yet her supposed superiors, the very gods who chastise my pastimes and mock my mother's mortality, were put to shame by this mere angel's better upbringing. She offered me food and drink before knowing my name, and I decided at once that we should be great friends.

"Uh, well, Honey, I think he was just leaving," hedged Cupid. "He gave me a lift home – as I'm injured." He pointed to his lacerated chest. "Maybe you noticed?"

"And I'm grateful he's taking care of you, looking the way you do." She gave him a pitying look. "I've got an ambrosia bath ready for you. I was told you'd need it."

"Told?" asked Cupid.

"Mmmm," replied his lady. "I'll explain later. While you clean up and change into something presentable, Bacchus can tell me all about your adventures, can't you?"

I smiled at her recognition of me. She really was well brought up.

Cupid frowned at the dismissal but turned toward the Great Room ahead and presumably the bath beyond.

Just as he cleared the room's entryway and turned left, I heard three barks in quick succession and frantic scratching on tiles. Cupid shouted from beyond my line of sight, and I saw the gleeful bounding – the blur, really – of a colossal, three-headed, black dog flash across the entry. Another shout and a loud crash later, and the dog burst into happy yips. The unmistakable swishing sound of a large, wagging tail followed. Cupid's lady laughed.

"Puppy does love Cupid."

"Is that his name? Puppy?" I asked.

"It's my little pet name for him. His real name's Cerberus, but I'm sure you know that."

I did, but I didn't wish to quiet her.

"I'm Tamara," she said modestly, as if every Olympian hadn't heard the tales of her heroism. Few in the Celestial City could claim to have saved the kingdom, and she and her band of friends most certainly could. The names Tamara, Tyrone, Jarel, Tommy, and Cornelius have become legend, and everyone knows that, without them, Cupid never could have saved the throne.

Tamara's heroism and hospitality were matched by her elegance. Her brown skin and graceful cheekbones were framed by shoulder-length, black, curly hair that reminded me of a black sand beach. I imagined us on a tropical island; it was a pretty little fantasy. Her powerful, golden wings were tinged with tiny red sparkles, and she wore a simple pink dress with three-quarter sleeves.

Nothing fancy. Absolutely perfect.

She led me to a sitting room to our right with a lovely servery in the corner. Her practiced hands poured the afternoon tea and served a generous portion of ambrosia cookies alongside. I liked her more with each passing moment. We spent the next ten minutes or so by my telling the tale of her beau's narrow escape from tropical waters and the jaws of his one-eyed kin. She was strangely calm, pulling a stray lock of hair behind an ear, not at all unsettled. I could tell she knew parts of my story already. At my coaxing, she told me a bit about her adventures in The Underworld, parts of which I also knew. But I could tell she had a new story to tell, and I could barely wait for Cupid to return so that I might hear it. (Few things please the god of theatre more than a juicy story.)

When Cupid did show himself again, the recovering playboy looked hardly worse for wear. The ambrosia bath did the trick to soothe the swelling and close the cuts. Cupid wore a light blue suit, the subtle coolness of which diminished the little remaining redness of his cheeks. If I had to guess, Tamara had laid it out for him for that purpose.

Cupid looked in my direction but didn't greet me. Instead, he sashayed up to Tamara and wrapped an arm around her shoulder. I heard his thoughts in my head: *See that, Bacchy? She's with me.*

(And people call *me* dramatic.)

"I'm glad you're feeling better, Darling," she said and turned to wrap her arms around his middle. She smiled up at him before releasing him. "Bacchus told me all about what happened. Clever escape. But you're going to have to figure out what's upset Triton and work out a truce. You can't avoid the open sea forever, and you did say you wanted to fly more and leave Tyrone to his own flights." She turned to address me. "Cupid would like him to earn status as a love angel himself. After Pluto's horrible fog, there's much more work to do on Earth than normal, and Tyrone is an excellent apprentice."

"I see," I answered smugly, laughing on the inside at Cupid's appalled thoughts: *She's not fawning! Why isn't she begging to help me through my suffering!*

Poor Tamara, I thought. *Dating a god means dealing with his tender sensibilities.* I knew better than her sweetheart, though; the girl recognized that his rash wasn't the biggest problem here.

Tamara bent to pick up her silver tray of cookies and offered some to Cupid. He took one and bit into it, realizing he needed a good amount of ambrosia to fight off the manchineel poison.

"Cupid?" she asked sweetly, returning the tray to the servery. "Do you have any idea why Morta would come to visit me?"

Cupid choked on the cookie and covered his coughs with his free hand. Color drained from his face.

He reached back with his cookied hand to find a place to sit. Feeling a chair, he plunked down onto it, preparing for the worst. "I have no idea, but–" he coughed a big one before clearing this throat forcefully – "I hoped to not see her again for millennia."

Morta, the cruelest and most feared of the Fates, the one who cuts a mortal's thread of life with her tapered, razor-sharp scissors, not only liked to flash her weaponry. She also liked to flaunt her wits and boast in complicated riddles. I couldn't wait to hear the latest. I grabbed another cookie.

"She didn't stay long, but she gave me a message." Tamara handed him a filled teacup. He emptied its contents in one gulp.

Cupid returned the teacup to its saucer amongst the set and dropped his head into his hands. He sighed loudly.

(Ha! This would be good!)

Tamara adjusted the sleeves of her pink dress. The color made her skin warmer and her dark brown eyes even darker. She could enchant anyone, and her sense of drama, I decided, may be her finest attribute.

"She said this, Cupid:

'To trade and deal is his heart's desire,
The still and slumbering night to mire
With dishonesty and covetous ire,

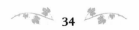

Turning favor toward himself, the liar.
You! Beware for your tenuous position.
A contender's undermining mission
May steal your courter, your swain some night.
'Tis stolen love – and vengeance right.'"

The room froze. Not a sound. Not a breath until Cupid finally blinked his now unswollen eyes and reopened them wide in fear. I would have remained still as a statue were I not compelled to quietly applaud in earnest reverence for such a momentous monologue. Her flawless recitation of lines, which she surely only heard once, for the Fates repeat nothing, could scarcely be expected of the greatest actresses in theatre's history.

Tamara shifted her eyes my way and nodded in acknowledgment of my ovation. She then returned her gaze toward Cupid and put her hands upon her hips.

"You've got some explaining to do, my love."

I sat back down for Act II's inevitable complication.

MANY PARTS

W hoa, whoa, whoa. I have no idea," Cupid answered with a hint of pleading in his voice.

"Hmmm, the still and slumbering night to mire," I repeated. "Who do we know who might mire slumbering nights?"

"What?" Cupid asked incredulously. "I didn't do anything." He waved his palms in front of him, and I couldn't help but think that those slightly ruddy hands had covered much territory on many ladies. One reaps what one sows. One cannot escape one's reputation, even through changed character, and I have no doubt that the same thought struck Tamara. She looked at her boyfriend.

"I never understand a thing the Fates say. I still don't understand now, even with the words coming out of *your* mouth. Your *gorgeous* mouth. The mouth I *treasure*, Honey."

I was impressed despite myself. Either Cupid was as good an actor as his lady is an orator or he genuinely didn't understand the poem – which *wouldn't* make him innocent of its accusations.

I sat on my hands to prevent any involuntary movements. A good and attentive audience must silently observe the performance unless courtesy demands a reaction. That wasn't the case here.

Tamara stood marbleized. Although her beguiling features hadn't transformed and her lovely face didn't threaten, the air hung heavy with suspicion. It was a delicious moment. Would that I could replicate it during each show I put to stage.

Cupid turned to face me and opened his arms in plea. "Bacchus! Bacchus, you tell her! You came to see me on the island, so you must have been watching me, maybe through your ERP, though I can't imagine why." *Weirdo,* he added silently.

The childish insult rang loud in my head. In my younger days, I might have reached my limit with Cupid's derisions, unspoken though they were. Now, however, as I sat at the precipice of a thrashing domestic drama and the lady deserved to hear what I'd already told her lover, I decided *not* to unleash my panthers on him (which would have made for a much *more* thrashing drama, I assure you) and instead chose to tighten the noose.

"Oh, but my wandering Cupid," I answered. "I only saw your actions of the past few hours. I know not what to tell the lady. But I can say to you that confession is good for the soul. As says The Bard," – and here I raised one arm in classic theatre pose – "'All the world's a stage, and all the men and women merely players. They have their exits and entrances, and one man in his time plays many parts.'" I lowered my hand and squinted suspiciously at my charge. "Are you playing many parts?"

Cupid tossed up his hands and stormed about the room, blathering about interfering oracles and angry sea gods and absent chauffeurs and jumping dogs and impossible workloads and poor character witnesses and why is Bacchus here anyway?

As he raged (in a manner that I imagined to be most unbecoming to the object of his courtship), the mistress of the house turned to me.

"I'm sorry you're having to see this, Bacchus, but, well, Cupid *is* the god of passion. Sometimes his emotions get hot. But as Cupid's guest, you're welcome to stay."

Cerberus suddenly bounded back into the Great Room. His giant bulk closed off its entrance to us sitting in the adjacent room. The hound stuck one of his snouts in and sniffed heartily. His flews flapped. His mouth dripped. His breath reeked.

Cupid stopped muttering and stomped up to him. Placing both hands onto the dog's wet, black nose, Cupid pushed and ordered him out. When the muzzle of "god's best friend" had cleared the entry, Cupid walked through the archway and clomped to his right, calling the dog to follow. A few heavy bounds, a door creaking open, a happy yip, and an exhausted "finally!" followed.

Ah, yes. Love is patient; love is kind.

Cupid returned wiping his hands on his trousers and leaving dark trails of snot. I certainly hoped he wasn't going to reach for more cookies. Tamara must have thought the same; she pushed the serving tray my way and stepped between us.

"Well, Bacchus?" Cupid finally demanded, leaning to one side to look past her. "What are you doing here? What's this all about?"

Tamara inhaled sharply, and I got the impression that she didn't like this confrontation – or the third degree turned toward me. However, in the interest of domestic tranquility, I answered.

"I've already told you, Cupid, but I suspect you weren't listening, concerned as you were with escape."

"What?" asked both Cupid and Tamara, she more politely than he.

"You'll recall," I said directly to Cupid, "being tied to the log? It was then that I told you."

"You babbled about melodramas and spotlights and the marvel of dry ice! And then you started praising Euripides and Miguel de Cervantes and George Bernard Shaw! I was about to get *eaten!* I didn't have time to hear you blow hot air about your silly entertainments!"

My anger spiked. Dry ice is supremely useful. And The God of Love calling Art silly! 'Tis more folly than to think infatuation a feeble force! Fittingly, the moment was punctuated by the fierce snarls of my panthers.

I stiffened to promote the idea that they had channeled my outrage (I was as good an actor as any.), but I knew their noise meant trouble; my cats only snarl for good reason.

Tamara put a calming hand upon both our forearms. Cupid's jaw dropped, and his brain unleashed a hundred hurtled profanities. Tamara turned as if she hadn't noticed his outrage. (The sly fox. I was liking her more and more by the second.) She addressed me with cool patience. "I missed that time you explained it, Bacchus, and Cupid is obviously still upset over how his day's gone. Would you repeat it, please?"

Peace is a woman's job, as the title goes, although, from the look of her athletic frame, I was sure Tamara wouldn't flee from a fight. Another snarl from outside distracted me for a half second, and I wondered if my cats needed attention, but, well, Tamara was my hostess and not to be ignored.

"Of course, m'lady," I replied with a slight bow. "I will repeat my tale for those who were either absent in their presence or present in their absence."

Cupid crossed his arms and huffed. A trio of barks resonated throughout the grounds. Cupid looked over his shoulder toward it but decided against missing my story a second time.

This time with an attentive audience, I recounted Mercury's intrusion into my dreams and his unfiltered access into others' unconscious minds. I left out the bits about hearing Cupid's thoughts and what I suspected

Mercury was up to – I couldn't accuse without proof nor would I risk destroying a mystery.

Tamara was an exemplary audience, motionless during the most critical moments of my tale and animated at the end. She even brought a hand to her mouth, as if fear required a gathering of strength. I must admit, had Cupid not staked his claim to her and made it known throughout Olympus, I might have tempted fate with an invitation to share an evening. I took her raised hand in my own and petted it in a show of compassion.

"I don't think you said any of that before," accused Cupid. (Did I mention that he's terribly inattentive?) "Anyway, none of that explains Triton or the Cyclops or Morta."

I released Tamara's hand, as I doubt she even noticed I was holding it. "Well," I answered reservedly, "to that I cannot speak. Yet."

A panther snarl and a resounding bark brought us all out of our pondering state. It was but a moment before the two sounds became many going back and forth, signaling a brawl.

"Oh, Puppy!" exclaimed Tamara, looking at Cupid in alarm. She rushed through the great room, and Cupid and I pursued her toward the back door, Cupid bellowing about overgrown pets. Bursting out and onto the grounds, we found Cerberus and my panthers tumbling in a furious pack. Each of Cerberus' heads was fighting one of my cats, which were scratching and biting, and they together were tearing up a milkweed patch on one side of the pond and generally acting as cats and dogs do toward each other.

I was supremely unconcerned because I knew my panthers could handle themselves and, in fact, it was good for them to occasionally see action. A tamed cat, you know, is hardly of any use. Plus, I saw three killed koi fish pond-side. My cats had been hunting. And fighting. Their version of drama.

"Cerberus!" scolded Tamara. The dog froze for her.

"Pantira!" I scolded, not because I meant it but because it would please the lady. My cats slunk toward the koi.

"My fish!" screamed Cupid. He rushed forward, I assume to save them, but it was too late, and his fear of panthers stopped him in his tracks. To save face, he turned and berated me. "Those koi are *my* pets! They're not food for yours!"

Tamara sighed. I imagine this is not the way house visits usually go. Cerberus was motionless but held a low growl. My pards leveraged their koi and began skinning them.

"I apologize, Cupid," I said and added a slight bow. "My cats have already taken your fish, but – " and here I shot a knowing glance toward Tamara, as I do always love conflict – "as you well know, there are plenty of fish in the sea."

Unless my ears deceived me, Cupid himself growled, lower and more quietly than Cerberus, but it was a growl nonetheless.

"I will gladly replace your fish," I offered, knowing full well that a pet is more than the animal.

"No," he said quickly (too quickly for his reply to be absent of meaning). He ran a hand up his long, sloping forehead and through his curly brown hair before sweeping it toward my chariot parked on an open patch beyond the opposite side of the pond. "I think it best if we just part ways. I'm sure you know the way out."

"O-o-o-o-o-h no," Tamara piped in. "I think Bacchus should stay awhile. He saw what happened this morning. If we go over it again, maybe we could find a clue about why." She turned to face me. "You'll stay, won't you?"

Who wouldn't, honestly?

I saw Cupid bristle and knew he'd made up my mind for me.

Chapter 6

A MITEY MESSAGE

I held out the nook of my elbow, and Tamara slid her arm in to guide me toward the house. As we walked, I looked back over my shoulder to ascertain the position of the animals but instead found Cupid a mere foot behind, keeping pace and glaring a hole through my skull. I leaned past him to spot my panthers, who were happily ripping apart fish flesh. Cerberus shifted to position himself between my cats and the pond, no doubt to block any more unauthorized snacking.

I looked forward again and pondered. Why Cupid was still angry was beyond me. I'd just told him the plot, offered to replace his fish, and essentially pledged a partnership just by being there. If he knew what I knew, he'd be so pleased with me as to run ahead to open the door.

Instead, as we climbed the lawn toward the castle, we saw a blue and white cherub darting like a nervous pinball within the open doorframe, up and down, side to side. The cherub had pointy, see-through, buggy wings, unlike the feathers of most cherubs. I recognized him instantly as Pip, a royal messenger.

Tamara's arm tensed in mine. After The Fates' warning, her apprehension was most warranted.

"Mr. Cupid!" the proctor heralded. "I've a message

from His Majesty King Jupiter!"

Tamara stopped dead in her tracks, as did I. That forced Cupid to collide into me, which had the unintended effect of making it look as if he was willing to knock us down to reach the courtly courier. He apologized and hurried to Tamara's other side.

Now what? I heard him think.

"Mr. Cupid," Pip said nervously by way of greeting.

"Inside," Cupid commanded. "I don't want to stand here watching or even hearing my fish being eaten."

Pip moved aside, and Cupid thrust open the door for all to pass. He then shuffled us off to a side room featuring an impressive bank of open windows facing the pond. Cupid turned his back to the beauty of it and crossed his arms. I suspect he positioned himself to force me to face it and thus witness my panthers' havoc. As my pets were happily fed, I instead chose to look around the parlor. It was smaller than the servery, painted a refreshing yellow, and lined by shelves piled high with scrolls, their edges sealed shut with red wax. I surmised that the scrolls were mere decoration as the seals remained unbroken. And I marveled at what secrets they might hold. Such is the mystery of literature. When I returned my gaze to my companions, I found the landed royalty among us awaiting Pip's message.

Pip flapped his buggy wings to remain at eye level yet lowered his own beady black eyes. I wondered if he was

contemplating an apology for past actions. Pip's enthu-
siasm to replace Cupid nearly ensured that Pluto pirated
all of Olympus.

"Um, sir," Pip began, raising his eyes to meet
Cupid's. "The Great King Jupiter requires a service of
you." (Ah, so no apology then. Instead he carries a godly
demand for more work. Typical.)

The minuscule messenger looked at Tamara and
me as if we were eavesdroppers. Now, I don't typically
expect non-gods like Pip to instantly drop to their feet
and grovel, but occasionally I feel the need to remind
sassy understudies just who is in charge of the production.
Messengers are not.

"Anything you say to me you may say in front of
Tamara," Cupid said, putting a reassuring arm around her.

"Thank you, Honey," Tamara said, returning the
embrace. She then turned toward Pip. "And any service
requested of my Cupid may be requested in front of Bacchus." She put her arm on my shoulder. (It was wonderful.
She smelled like candy.) "Bacchus has proven himself to
be a friend."

Cupid did not deserve such a prize. The look on
his face said he didn't feel he deserved anything like what
was happening.

The cherub rallied and spoke. "Mr. Cupid, His
Majesty King Jupiter was impressed with the way you
fought for his kingdom. He particularly mentioned your

cunning and devotion."

"Hold everything," interrupted Cupid with a raised hand. He looked irked. "You saw Jupiter, and he said this to you?"

"Yes, sir."

Cupid glared. "Why didn't he call me up to his palace himself?"

"Because no one sees Jup-"

"Pip," Tamara interrupted. "We all saw Jupiter at the Colosseum."

"Yes, the king of the gods does show himself, but only rarely," Pip answered, not quite showing the same servile attitude toward Tamara as he had Cupid. "His Majesty prefers to see rather than to be seen. I believe he makes his absence part of his mystique."

Cupid waved a hand in disgust. Pip, that little bug, looked around for permission to finish delivering his message. Tamara nodded. I would have burped in his face as my consent but never in front of the lady.

"As I was saying, sir," Pip went on, turning toward Cupid. "Your deeds did not go unnoticed. He especially... er, *appreciated*, shall we say ... your willingness to bend laws for the overall good of the kingdom."

Cupid's brows furrowed in confusion.

"Jupiter was pleased that you were willing to do anything, even break into Olympus, even steal from his palace and your own, to keep the kingdom safe."

(Stagehands, this is your cue. Lower the white lights and brighten the red. When a god's pleased that you've been a sneaky snake, that means he's found his abettor; a feeling of unease crawled its hundred legs all over me. Blast the overhead fans for a mere moment. Let the audience feel an unmistakable change around them.)

"I suspected that it was you, sir, who trampled me that day at the base of Jupiter's stairs. You escaped, but Jupiter somehow knew it was you. He believes you to be an adept thief, and so our lord asks that you again show your loyalty."

This Pip had us still as statues – and he wasn't even a good speaker.

"Jupiter has intelligence of a plot against himself and Her Majesty Queen Juno. The plot involves Vulcan, sir. Only this time, Vulcan's trap wouldn't confine the queen to her throne. Rather, it would keep both members of the royal couple away from their thrones forever. Vulcan intends to capture them to keep them out because, well, as we all know, were the royal couple off their thrones but for a day..."

"The ensuing power struggle would be spectacular," I finished his sentence.

Pip ignored the interruption. "A destabilized

Olympus means little to no heavenly work gets done. Earth eventually falls into chaos. Jupiter, of course, must prevent that, but diplomacy demands that he not straightforwardly attack Vulcan. Jupiter contends that Vulcan's crown is key somehow, and so, Mr. Cupid, Our Lord asks that you steal it."

Tamara gasped. Cupid balked. I practically squealed in delight. What an impertinent request! It would be perilous. Nearly impossible. Possibly suicidal. Yet adventurous – and, as Aesop says, "Adventure is worthwhile!"

"And Mr. Cupid, no one must know that you are working on his behalf. No one."

Cupid, Tamara, and I looked at each other. Vulcan, the Lord of Lode and Lava, the king of fire and volcanoes and metalwork, would not take kindly to anyone entering his domain, especially thieves after his crown. And Vulcan is renowned for his cunning traps. His smithy would be booby-trapped and deathly dangerous.

I looked at Tamara, who lowered her head and whispered to herself, "'A contender's undermining mission may steal your courter, your swain some night.'" She repeated Morta's warning. "''Tis stolen love...'" she went on. Cupid brought a hand to his forehead. I stifled a snide grin; far be it from me to suppress a quest.

Tamara looked up. "Cupid, this fight is right."

Chapter 7

INDUCTEES

Cupid turned to me with deep trepidation. As well he should. Vulcan is no chump. He and I are friendly acquaintances, although I haven't seen him in some time. He's the sort of god one doesn't want to visit unless it is absolutely necessary. Imposing on Vulcan's self-imposed hermitage, making a pest of yourself, is most unwise. Allow me an explanatory exposition:

Many, many centuries ago, Jupiter and Juno had their only legitimate male child, he who would become heir to the kingdom. But when the child was born, Juno saw what had come from her marital union: an infant she deemed so ugly, she felt justified in hurling him to the sea. (Who was the ugly one in *that* situation, I ask you?)

The boy's impact from such a height caused his legs to snap; other parts shifted and bent. His could have been a terrible fate, but we can thank a friendly sea-nymph for saving his life and rearing him, humpbacked and lame as he was destined to be, into Vulcan, one of the most talented and industrious gods ever. Do not believe, reader, that Vulcan would have grown to be as persevering and formidable had he grown up in that overly-soft cloud fortress in the sky. Fate is fickle.

When Vulcan grew and eventually learned of his

lineage and his mother's cruel rejection, he brought his craftiness to bear and created a most ingenious chair. It was booby-trapped, of course, and so when Juno pridefully sat her royal derrière upon the new, beautifully artisaned throne, the chair sprung to avenging action and held her fast. She could not escape its grasp.

Unable to break its spell and despairing for his wife's eternity, Jupiter called upon me to fetch Vulcan. I fancy myself an eager conversationalist and friendly drinking companion, but Vulcan was not easily swayed. He knew that he had succeeded in subjecting his mother to both a handicap mimicking his own and retribution for her abandonment. He had won.

Still, after sharing much wine and spending a few days in friendly banter, I asked Vulcan very nicely that he reconsider. (I think most people respond well to amiable conversation and niceties.) With my oratory skills and, of course, my exquisite wine, I was able to convince Vulcan to show compassion and go up to Mount Olympus.

When we arrived, Jupiter offered Vulcan a bribe – er, a reward – to release Juno. He awarded Venus as a bride. That was another ugly act, to be sure, but such is the privilege of kings. Interestingly, the goddess of love and beauty did not seem to object. Perhaps opposites really do attract. Or perhaps she simply wanted a man that she wouldn't have to guard against infidelity as much as he does she. Vulcan and I shared one more drink after he brought her home, and I left them to their marital bliss. Vulcan and I have been friends ever since.

"Bacchus?" asked Tamara, pulling me from my reverie and shaming me for having gotten lost in thought in front of such sweet company.

"Yes, my dear?" I answered thoughtlessly, perhaps revealing too much of my inner thoughts. Cupid glared.

"You and Vulcan are friends, aren't you? That's the story anyway. What are the chances he'd just surrender the crown on Jupiter's request if you asked?"

"No chance whatsoever – my dear," I quickly added, re-using the term of endearment that had riled Cupid – specifically to rile him. "Vulcan is possessive of his belongings, or, shall we say, whatsoever he feels is rightfully his. Certainly his crown would fit that category. He would neither surrender it nor leave it out for the taking, and, in fact, it would be well protected. I've never even seen it. Also, Vulcan is a top trapper. If one required proof, one would need look no further than his marital history with Venus, of which I'm sure you're both very well familiar."

Allow me another exposition, if you please, before I continue our tale. This one is for your benefit, dear reader, I promise:

Shortly after Vulcan's marriage to Venus, Apollo, the sun god (who is my half-brother and Mercury's, too; we're all Jupiter's sons by union outside of marriage), who sees all as he drives his sun chariot across the sky, informed Vulcan of Venus' many clandestine meanderings around the globe. Apollo hinted at romantic rendezvous.

The legends say that Vulcan boiled with anger and vowed to humiliate anyone trying to make him the fool. Today Vulcan is rather known for catching the gods in their most excellent moments of misbehavior and hypocrisy, and this is the preeminent example why.

Vulcan, The King of Coal, intended to catch his wayward bride and eradicate her unknown lover. Metal Master as he is, he wove a net of steel so gossamer thin as to be nearly invisible to the naked eye and so wickedly ensnaring as to tighten the more its captives struggled. Vulcan carefully hung the net over his marriage bed and announced a day trip to a volcano on the other side of the globe. It was a ruse. Instead, he withdrew from his cavernous home to travel to the homes of friends, whom he then invited to become audience to a public humiliation for the ages. Only, when Vulcan's lookout reported seeing a visitor slinking into his underground lair, and Vulcan and his accompanying witnesses swooped in for the big reveal, who did they find ensnared but Venus and Vulcan's own brother, Mars?

Ho, ho, ho! The outrage! The earthquakes! The fire and brimstone! They say even mighty Mars, god of war, trembled at the savagery of Vulcan's venom.

But Venus did not. She ... lovely she, enchanting

she, beguiling she ... demurely covered her exposed body with her dainty hands and sweetly stared into the eyes of her zealous, jealous husband, somehow securing the attention of the entire room and quieting earthquakes the world over. (Would that I could have been there.) Only Venus' skill in tempering a man's temper saved the adulterous pair – and the life of their resultant son, Lover Boy here. Cupid, by being the son of Venus and Mars, by the mere act of being born, was historically hamstrung to be Vulcan's shame and enemy.

If I hadn't known for sure that the mental doorway between us only swung one way, I'd have thought by the look on Cupid's face that he could read my mind. But I knew he couldn't. If he could, he'd be running. No, he was merely contemplating Venus' marital history with Vulcan. She – and her lover – were released unharmed thanks to Vulcan's devotion to her. Cupid, were he to be caught in Vulcan's lair, would be provided no such sanctuary. The blood draining from Lover Boy's face revealed that he knew it, too.

"I repeat that His Majesty wishes this to be a secret mission. Lady Venus is not to be consulted or warned. Jupiter's name is not to be breathed." Pip puffed out his chest; the bovarist spiked my irritation.

"I'd like to speak to Jupiter about this myself," Cupid said.

"No time," Pip replied. "Our intelligence indicates

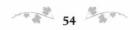

that Vulcan will spring his trap tomorrow night at Jupiter's anniversary ball. The crown must be yours before then."

Ah, the anniversary ball, a gala event wherein our leader, Jupiter, pretends to honor the date of his wedding. It's a masked ball, of course, so that all of his *secret* mistresses can remain incognito, their attendance impelled by their fear of his wrath. There'll be no *known* mistresses in attendance, they having been summarily dispatched by his justifiably furious wife as soon as she learns of them. The ball is a well choreographed dance of hypocrisy.

"But a day and a half is plenty of time for me to see Jupiter," replied Cupid. "And I could even get Jarel to help. He knows how to 'get' things."

"He's training with your father, Honey," Tamara said, "as you should well remember, to be the next apprentice to the god of war."

I heard Cupid's thoughts cloud with anger and jealousy before asking her, "Do you know what he told me on the very first day we met?"

She shook her head.

"He told me he dislikes confrontation. Yet here he is training with my father. My father, the warlord! One little scrabble in the Safe House and suddenly Dad thinks that Jarel's the next best thing for warfare since ballistics."

The group was losing its thread. I cleared my throat, and Cupid returned to the matter at hand. "As I was saying, Pip, there's plenty of time for me to see Jup--."

"His orders are to start immediately," interrupted Pip, clearly irritated at the delay. I was within seconds of dashing him to dust. The absolute gall to interrupt a god – even a meandering one! And then demand that he spring to action!

"Hold on," Cupid said before turning to Tamara. "Don't you find it odd that I'd be sent out on a mission to steal? And by my grandfather who never seems to want to see me? And he never invites me to the ball. Where is it this year, Pip?"

"Australia. The Sydney Opera House."

"Oooh," I cooed involuntarily. Sydney's performing arts center is one of the world's premier artistic venues. It showcases not only magnificent opera but also superb theatre, heartbreaking ballet, and moving orchestra performances to rival any city in the world. It is one of my most favorite haunts.

I turned to see Cupid staring at me with furrowed-brow annoyance.

"As I was saying," he said irritably, "Jupiter asks me to steal from another god? And right in the middle of this Triton trouble? And now suddenly Vulcan is plotting?"

That caused me pause. I would not have suspected that Vulcan still harbored resentment, but I suppose it's hard to know the inner thoughts of a god who spends nine tenths of his day pounding metal underground.

"Well, Cupid," answered Tamara slowly, "as Morta

warned about someone trying to take you from me, I'm worried about all those things, yes, but we can't learn anything about any of it by staying here. Maybe Triton is acting as a diversion for Vulcan. It's not like all the gods don't have axes to grind one way or the other."

I allowed her impertinence as it rang truer than anything said in the room thus far.

"I think it's right that you go. That *we* go." She added quickly upon seeing him shake his head vehemently, "We make a good team. And I'd like Bacchus to come along as well." She directed her next words at me. "You've helped Jupiter and Juno before, and it seems like they need it again. If you'd be willing to join us and sway Vulcan if we get caught, we'd be forever grateful. Would you, Bacchus?"

A company of chorus angels never sounded sweeter. The gratitude of a near goddess and the promise of death-defying drama? It was my nectar as surely as ambrosia.

"Of course, my dear. I'd be honored to assist. And, Pip," I called, turning to the little speck who'd suddenly risen high on my list of disliked types, "I insist that you come along."

The floating splotch of a being gasped and waved his hands to protest, I'm sure, of his high position as messenger or manager or whatnot, employing whatever excuse practiced by those useless higher-ups who delegate all the work to those talented beings under their thumbs, but I wasn't about to miss this opportunity to add to our ranks and annoy Cupid in one fell swoop. I interrupted Pip's babbling – as is the right of a god to a lesser, not the other way around.

"I don't go unless Pip goes," I said.

"And we don't go unless Bacchus does," Tamara agreed.

Cupid and Pip both blanched. Neither wanted to go and certainly not with each other, if Cupid's thoughts were to be believed. But we'd given them no choice. I wanted Pip, that offensive little snot, to have to get his hands dirty before daring to interrupt a god again, and Tamara wanted the assurance of more help. We were in agreement again, albeit with slightly differing motivations.

Pip sighed. Cupid echoed.

And Tamara and I knew we'd won.

Chapter 8

DRESS REHEARSAL

As Jupiter had demanded an immediate departure, I stepped aside and held out a hand to summon my thyrsus.

Oh, no, Cupid thought (and I heard).

Oh, yes, I silently replied. So far, Tamara had seen me enter her home much less dramatically than her injured lover; I demanded considerably less attention than he (All I required were a few cookies and a baffling prophesy.), and I behaved staidly. Thus, lest Tamara find my company dull, I decided it was time to display some theatrical prowess of my own.

I spied my thyrsus hurtling toward me and lunged to one side just as it soared through an open window. Nabbing it midair, I caught a thrill flash through Tamara's eyes and wasn't about to waste it.

Continuing my one fluid motion, I swung the rod like a scythe over my head before lowering it to point toward my chariot. The rod's end flashed white, brightening to blinding. I watched the yard, ready for the show.

My chariot quivered. The ivy leaves engraved along its edges slithered and popped free from their two-dimensional depiction, eager to assist me, but I raised a finger to stay them. I required their brethren. My celestial tools, cast in the silver relief sculpture at the base of the chariot's walls, heaved as breath itself. They pulled away from the home that protected them against age and theft, the home given to me by Vulcan, the only god with skill enough to cast soft silver without stronger copper. I would not betray Vulcan without reason.

I watched as my celestial tools revealed themselves within the theatrical scene complete with stage, props, and regalia just visible behind a withdrawn curtain. The tools broke the confines of the sheltering silver, transformed to their real-world states, and sped my way. I was delighted to see them, as one greets lifelong friends: my ambrosia tray (made from twisted fig tree wood), my perpetually refilling wine goblet (which I rarely make use of, as grape is so easy to find worldwide), and an orb as big as Cupid's head (but certainly not as large as his ego). I could have summoned all these tools without the blinding lightshow, but my flash had so much more … *flash*.

Showoff, Cupid thought.

"Oooooh, what's that?" Tamara asked. I knew the orb especially would work on the one I'd hoped to impress. It rarely fails to fascinate with its swirling glaze as white as milk.

"A gift from the huntress Diana."

"Will we need it?" interjected Pip.

The shrew needs taming, I thought, *never mind that he's male.* I refrained for the third time in probably as many minutes from ridding myself of the termagant termite. Not normally so easily roused, I quelled my tempest to realize the importance of being earnest.

"Of course we'll need it," Tamara answered. "Bacchus wouldn't have summoned it otherwise." She turned to face me. "Please, what is it?"

"Some time ago," I explained, "I was in the Galician woodlands of Northern Spain where I had stopped to water my panthers. I discovered along the stream a patch of dying vegetation. Anyone who appreciates plants, like, say, a god of wine, knows that one bad patch of vegetation can infect another, and so I waved my thyrsus over it to withdraw its poison. Little did I know that my half-sister – another of Jupiter's children born out of wedlock – had been watching. Diana cares for her sacred forests and wildlife as much as her twin brother, Apollo, tends to the sunshine needed to feed them. As thanks for protecting the wildwood, Diana presented me with this rather luminous sphere."

"What does it do?" Tamara persisted.

"Touch it," I answered.

"What?! No! That's crazy!" interjected Cupid, but his dearie had already trusted my suggestion. Her unpainted fingernail touched the magical ball, and its surface swirled to reveal Earth's landmasses without any cities to sully them. From the landmasses sprouted minuscule mountains and caves, trees and streams, deserts and dunes.

She stared, enthralled.

"It's a living map of the world's unspoiled places," I explained, "and of the spoiled ones as they once were."

"Caves might be unspoiled, but Vulcan's mines certainly aren't," squawked the scourge of my patience. "His furnace burns red day and night. What good could that globe possibly do us?"

I can't stand that little-" thought Cupid. I never felt so in league with him.

"Pip!" scolded Tamara. "None of us can speak to each other like that on this trip. We have to get along. Now apologize."

(Stagehands, turn the spotlight to the leading lady and dim the back lights to a gentle pink while I think my many adoring thoughts for this fabulous female. Although that could last hours, let us sustain the light but briefly.)

Pip frowned and was silent a second longer than he should have been but must have realized his rudeness. "Sorry," he mumbled.

Unreal, Cupid thought. *She actually got that zit to zip it.*

Tamara looked at me, and I tipped my head ever so slightly at Pip to acknowledge his apology. He *was* a little zit. "A globe is ever useful," I replied simply.

I suddenly sensed a great deal of aging wild vine

on the outskirts of Cupid's property, and so I summoned it forth with a flick of the wrist. In moments, it frantically wiggled through the open windows, wrapped itself around my celestial gear, and looped up and over to create straps. I hoisted my new biological backpack onto my back and, using my thyrsus as a walking stick, was ready for a miles-long trek underground.

Cupid summoned his own ambrosia tray and his famed bow and quiver. Pip blathered about the countless things he needed to retrieve from his residence, a tiny room in Jupiter Heights. I silenced him with a glare. Tamara excused herself to change, and Cupid followed suit.

She returned in a plain black, three-quarter sleeve shirt, khaki pants, and black boots, very suitable for the start of a mission. She slung her small silver bow and quiver over her shoulders, and I was reminded that she was quickly becoming one of the most prolific and accurate love angels in Olympus. It was a mystery why Jupiter ever let her and her hundreds of fallen-angel coworkers go.

Cupid returned in a grey T-shirt and matching pants and shoes. No pizzazz, but no matter. He slung a much larger and more elaborately carved and bejeweled bow over his shoulder along with his famed ever-filling quiver. I wondered if Tamara's quiver had such accommodations. I looked down at my brown dress shoes, dark green suit, lilac shirt, and deep purple handkerchief. Such an outfit is always right.

We walked outside. My panthers hitched themselves to the chariot and followed us as we walked toward the front of the castle. Cerberus stayed back to protect the pond. It was just as well; he'd be too big to come along.

The late evening sun was starting to dip, Apollo being nearly done with his day's work. No matter. Once we entered Vulcan's lair, daylight would be irrelevant.

When we reached the front lawn, Cupid turned to Pip. "I hope you know what we're in for, what Jupiter asked for. Outside of the palace, life's a lot harder."

And it will be worse if we're caught, I thought. If Cupid thinks Triton's puny, petulant waves are chancy, wait 'til he sees Vulcan's fury.

Chapter 9

ASSUMING COMMAND

Pip wasted not a moment to assert himself. "Everyone knows that Vulcan's lair is under Mount Aetna, so I say we go there directly. Bacchus, Tammy, and I will go in the chariot, and since there's no more room, Cupid, you can fly alongside."

Tamara was the first to react – probably because Cupid and I were too stunned to believe Pip's audacity.

"Whoa, whoa, whoa!" Tamara interjected, wagging a finger in front of her face.

I suddenly realized the gravity of insisting Pip come along. It was a prelude to murder. Either Cupid or I would strangle him.

"I am *not* Tammy. I am Tamara. And we aren't anywhere near close enough for you to call me nicknames or determine my travel partn-"

Cupid stepped on her words and hurled profanities at Pip that I didn't realize a love god would know. And then *I* stepped on *Cupid's* stream of insults to remind Pip that he, bacillus that he is, was there as *our* helper and not the other way around. I allowed my thyrsus to glow red in anger. My panthers, seeing it, roared urgently.

Pip turned from whitish blue to baby pink, and I wondered if he wasn't embarrassed or perhaps revealing some heretofore unknown power. He raised his hands in defeat.

"I thought it was a good idea," he answered lamely.

"There can only be one leader of this group, Pip," said Cupid. "Me."

I admit that I'm not a skilled enough actor to have portrayed surprise.

"But Bacchus can-" Tamara began.

Cupid raised a quieting hand. "I don't appreciate Pip's assumption that I can't handle this. As far as I know, there are only two of us here who've broken into other gods' palaces. You and me. So we're the only ones ready for the job. But Jupiter put this quest on *me*. He sought my particular skills for the job, and in the end I'm the one who'll have to answer to him, so I'm in charge."

Tamara pursed her lips, but didn't argue. It was the loudest silence I'd ever heard.

And I was suddenly struck by how different this Cupid was from the earlier diapered one.

Cupid turned toward me. "I certainly don't have any experience with Vulcan as I've spent my entire life avoiding him. There's no sense reminding him of my mom's unfaithfulness by flaunting myself in his presence. Tamara clearly hasn't had any contact with him, judging by the questions she asked you. And if Pip had anything to do with him, I'd guess it was in his official capacity as royal messenger. But you, Bacchus? Yeah, you were

Vulcan's friend and you'll know more about him than all of us, and so I ask for your help, but in the end everyone needs to understand that, in this instance, I'm the heavy."

I was momentarily flummoxed by his rare show of logic.

And being a bad boy thief can't hurt my reputation any, Cupid added silently in his head.

Ha! I knew his chutzpa wouldn't let me down. Still, he was right, and I was pleased. My turn.

(Stagehands, transition to a spotlight and cast the scenery in shadow for my masterful monologue.)

"I wouldn't dream of undermining your leadership," I lied. (Of course I would. Drama demands it.) I went on. "If you seek my guidance, I advise opposite Pip."

Pip pouted. I went on. "We certainly cannot embark by traveling directly to Mt. Aetna. Obviously, Vulcan will have that well guarded and protected against intruders. He is the blacksmith of the gods, after all. His smithy is home to secrets and weaponry of unimaginable power. He created Jupiter's thunderbolt. He vivified servants made of gold. Not only do Vulcan's sentinels scan the skies, but his machinations certainly mind the mountain. A direct approach is foolhardy in the extreme.

"However, I know something about his forge home that few do. I learned it while plying his compassion to release Juno. Next to his worktable, which we converted to a makeshift bar to better enjoy our time of camaraderie, was a wellspring of lava that bubbled at ground level. I remember it distinctly because I feared that if either of us got too drunk, we might stumble and fall into it. I was sure such a tumble wouldn't affect Vulcan in the slightest. But me, full of high-proof spirits as I was, I would burst right into flames, and so I kept an eye on the spring.

As Vulcan lamented his tragic tale, crying into his drink – proving the old saying, *in vino veritas*, with wine comes truth – I watched lava bubbles slowly rise in the well. They'd pop with a hiss, expelling heat and steam, and then the lava would drift outward toward the edges of the wellspring, blackening as it cooled, only to break away and flare once more. It was mesmerizing. And as I watched, something unexpected happened. Chunks of black rock and a square of parchment rose from the lava depths and rested at the top of the bubbling puddle.

"The rocks held no interest for me, of course, as they undoubtedly weighted down the parchment until it was called up, but that parchment! It fascinated me. It was obviously enchanted to not burn. A quick glance at it revealed the lines and annotations of blueprints. I assumed the plans were highly secret, as they were hidden in such a way until their master appeared. They being so supremely secret, and their master still crying his tale of woe, I took a good, long look at them before they descended back into the lava. The plans depicted a tunnel from Vulcan's underground home in eastern Sicily to Venus' hilltop day-spa temple in Western Sicily."

My audience stood rapt, and I admit that I reveled in my performance.

(Lights up for the continued action.)

Again Tamara reacted first.

"So there's a secret passage between the two homes. That's probably clear of booby traps as it's meant for just them. But how do we get to Venus' temple? I mean, Venus' home will be guarded, too, as she has quite a few admirers who would love to find her at her own place away from her husband."

Cupid lowered an eyebrow.

"Yes, my dear," I answered. "It would be most unwise to believe that the skies around Venus' temple are unguarded. That's why we will need to get to her castle through yet another secret way. And here's where Diana's Orb has another use."

I handed Tamara my thyrsus, removed my backpack, and pulled out the Orb from within. Holding it at eye level, I blew onto it. Landmasses appeared and a hollow vein of cave began to distinguish itself, glowing slightly yellow and pulsating like a cautioning stoplight set at a quarter brightness.

"There it is. The cave starts deep underwater at the base of the sheer Sicilian rockface. From there it's more or less a 45-degree angle up to the Castello di Venere, the Castle of Venus."

"What?" Cupid asked incredulously, his brows steepling above his nose. "I've been to my mom's castle a thousand times, and I've never seen a cave leading to the sea or anywhere else. Besides, how do you figure that Vulcan won't have that one protected as well?" The dim, helpless darling.

"Oh, I highly doubt Vulcan knows about it, Cupid," I poo-pooed. "Think about it."

He huffed, and I heard him struggle. When Tamara smiled to my left, I invited her to share her conclusion.

"Don't you see, Sweetheart? The cave goes away from Vulcan and toward a place where few could survive: the deep sea. Your mom was made from the sea, so she can survive exiting and entering that cave very easily."

Yeah, so? he asked silently.

"She probably excavated the cave herself as an escape launch, a way to leave her castle without her husband knowing." She turned toward me. "Venus probably carved it out right after the Mars incident, wouldn't you say?"

I nodded. Tamara really was as wise as she was charming.

"How can we be sure of that?" demanded Pip.

"We can't – until we are," answered Tamara with

the recklessness of someone determined to ward off fateful warnings about lost loves.

"Whoa, hey now," said Cupid, finally cottoning on. "You want us to sneak in that way?! I don't wanna go anywhere near water, much less dive into the deep sea! Triton'll send a super sea squid or something; it'll try to crack me in half like a lobster tail!"

"Darling, don't be silly," chided Tamara. "How will he possibly know we're there?"

"He'll send sentinels out to patrol the seas! He'll have plankton nark about my whereabouts! He'll have starfish sniff me out! How in Gorgons' gills am I supposed to know his methods of detection?"

"But, Cupid," she went on, "even if he does somehow learn of our presence, we'll be safely inside your mom's castle before he can do a thing about it."

Cupid shook his head. "Maybe, but I don't like it. You don't know what I just went through." He turned toward me. "There's gotta be another way."

I sighed, sympathetic. "The skies are out. It's an island, so unless we're prepared to bore deep into the earth's crust to burrow through land plates, land's out. Water seems to be the only way."

Cupid put his hands to his eyes and rubbed hard. I heard his troubled thoughts. *Dangerous. Risky.*

"I'm willing to try, Cupid," Tamara said.

Of course you are, Cupid thought. *You're scared of*

The Fates' prophesy and you haven't seen Triton yet.

My dramatic instincts, which aren't always in line with self-preservation, agreed that testing the cave's accessibility without weeks of planning was rather reckless, but we didn't have weeks. On the plus side, this would be a grand way to enliven the next few days.

Cupid shook his head, not at all liking the plan but having no better one to supplant it. I took advantage of his stupefaction to step into my chariot. Tamara and Pip looked to Cupid for a verdict, and when he gave up thinking and slowly stepped in the chariot, they followed.

Chapter 10

THE PITCH

D espite Pip's gloomy earlier prediction, we all fit in easily.

The cats latched onto the chariot's reins for a fast, easy pull to the western side of Sicily. From afar, the island looked like a deflated soccer ball wasting away at the toe of Italy's boot. Getting nearer, one could see the beauty of the place. It held its challenges, however; the churning sea buffeted its western face.

"Don't worry, my dear," I said at Tamara's concerned look. "Most cats detest water, but panthers positively love it and are excellent swimmers."

I raised my head and called out to my pards, who turned their heads to better hear.

"Grab hold, everyone. We dive as far in as the cats can fight the water pressure. When the water wins, we shake loose the chariot and swim for the cave. My thyrsus will show us the way."

"Wait! We need a better plan than that!" Cupid shouted, but my panthers, obeying me and me alone, saw Tamara grab hold of my arm in preparedness and my nod of approval. They plummeted down.

Pip shrieked and flew into the foot space of the chariot, hoping for a brace against the quickly approaching water. The waves churned violently below us.

Cupid whirled his hands overhead and conjured a freshwater bubble around the chariot, encapsulating air and presumably easing the cats' swim. The sea mass grew larger and the crests fiercer as we neared. Tamara gasped before holding her breath. Pip screamed.

"Tamara, don't wait for me!" Cupid urged.

And the chariot smashed into the sea.

Experiencing a plunging high dive is a lot like passing out drunk. You fleetingly lose your senses, and then, when you come out of it, you're stunned. Cupid's bubble kept the seawater from completely blinding or freezing us, but the darkness that enveloped us after the initial shock of entry was worse than stunning. It invoked a terror of the crushing weight of leagues of sea.

I hit the end of my thyrsus against the chariot floorboard, and light burst from it into the gloom. My panthers pumped their legs so hard that their backs rose and fell like waves themselves. They were fighting the water well, but we'd have only seconds.

"Prepare yourselves," I warned and wrapped my arm around Tamara's waist. "Take another deep breath, and I'll be sure to get you to the safety of the cave."

Cupid didn't protest. Strangely, he wasn't cursing me in his mind. It was only when I looked to him that I noticed that he wasn't even looking our way.

Pandora's Box! I heard him think, and in my mind's eye, I saw through his: twenty or so mermen just coming out of the pitch, charging toward us. Their angry, piercing eyes held a still line while their huge tails rose and dipped behind them. They were swimming a lot faster than we were, and we were about to lose our chariot.

I whistled, the cats shook themselves loose, and Cupid's fresh-water air bubble collapsed under the weight of the sea.

Chapter 11

FISH BAIT

Frigid water beset us. Its brine sandpapered our skin and buffeted us with buoyancy. The sea wanted to push us up, but we needed to go down, even though plowing through such thick, salty water would have been extremely difficult for even the most athletic beings. (Good thing that my cats are extremely athletic; do you see why I refuse to domesticate them?)

With Tamara clutched to my chest, I thrust my thyrsus forward even as my panthers turned to face the mermen. They had not seen this welcome party through me, for I have no such mind connection to my cats as through Cupid. I assume they merely caught a whiff of fish. Their favorite.

My thyrsus flashed white in warning and suddenly yanked us through the water as if we'd latched onto a dolphin. Tamara buried her face into my neck, likely to avoid the harsh friction of current against her face. A shallow god might have enjoyed her cozying up; I was that shallow god.

I worried for a moment for my companions, Cupid and Pip, but quickly disavowed myself of any guilt for having left them. They were a god and a celestial emissary, respectively, and should be able to handle themselves.

Tamara, on the other hand, was neither a god nor an official ambassador, and my quixotic nature demanded chivalry.

But as we rushed through the ever-heavier waters, Cupid's terror sliced through my mind. I felt his eyes widen and saw through his vision a heavily muscled man-fish pointing a coral sceptre directly at him. It had to be the lead merman. His skin was green and grey and as heavily striped as a tiger's pelt. His hair was as dark and flat as seaweed and adorned with shells, shark teeth, and what looked like bullet casings. The half-fish opened his mouth to reveal jagged teeth and to disgorge a bloodcurdling cry, like the sound an animal of the sea might make upon its slaughter – if it could.

Cupid tried in vain to gather water before he realized yet again that salt water would never obey him if Neptune disallowed it. The balneal being would *not* allow it, Cupid concluded (again, later than I would have), so he decided that the best tactic was to turn tail and swim.

I shook Cupid's sights from my mind and looked ahead into the Cimmerian shade in which we were all trapped. A form appeared, the jagged but much-welcome rockface, with a dark spot demarcating the entrance to a cave. My thyrsus focused its energy toward it.

Cupid intruded in my mind again against my will. I needed to help Tamara, yet Cupid's struggle was real. He swam as hard as he could, but the water seemed to fight him more than others. Pip was advancing ahead of him, but his tiny limbs and wings would never win the battle before his air ran out.

Cupid's determination pierced me. He willed himself forward and grabbed Pip just as the merman behind him screamed again – this time in fear. Cupid turned his head to see the merman suddenly jerk away from him. The manfish flailed and screamed as the scariest panther (in Cupid's mind) pulled him away and shook him like a chew toy. The other mermen broke their charge, terror streaking across their black eyes. They'd never seen a black panther, I was sure. To them, my cat was a sea monster.

The mermen scrambled to create distance, colliding with each other in the process. I watched with satisfaction as my alpha panther ripped away his merman's lower half.

My thyrsus slammed to a halt. We'd reached the black hole of the cave, and again I shook away Cupid's visions to do my own rescuing. I quickly but reluctantly peeled Tamara from my chest and pointed. Without hesitation, she swam into the mouth of the cave, her feet quickly disappearing upward. She would be safe, and, importantly, I noted, she trusted me in that.

I stabbed the ground end of my thyrsus into a crevice in the rock and turned to help my brethren. I took only a few, difficult strokes, which endangered my oxygen supply, when five figures burst out of the darkness and into the encircling light.

To the left was Cupid, riding one of my panthers

like a cowboy breaking a bronco: one arm around its neck
and the other wrapped around Pip like a child might hold
a doll – and Pip looking desperately grateful for the ride.

To the right were my two other panthers, the alpha
with part of a mertail in his mouth and the other – to
borrow a military phrase – "getting his six."

Realizing I had only seconds, I flip-turned to lead
them to the cave. They were coming in fast and hard. The
remaining merbrigade was almost upon us. (Stagehands, stack the many mer-actors high
and wide on wires across the backdrop.
Take up the entire back curtain with this
charging army.)

I thrashed toward the rockface. My hands auto-
matically reached for my thyrsus, but I realized in that
instant that it would hinder us. I left it and heaved myself
into the grotto and upward.

I was running out of air. I felt my head spin. I
wondered who might weave "Some Pig" at the threat of
my demise. Alas, I have no Charlotte nor her web.

In my mind's eye, I saw Cupid thrusting Pip into
the cavity and pushing him upward as Cupid himself frantically rose up the chute. He turned to watch the cats and
thought, *"Thank the gods for them!"*

He's learning, I thought.

I saw through Cupid's eyes as the omega cat turned
to swipe the webbed fingers groping after him.

The mermen did not pursue, and for the life of me, I didn't know why. They would have caught us in the incline, of that I was sure. But as we swam and clawed and climbed our way up the rock tunnel, and as I was convinced we'd never make it to the top, I felt the water change. It lost its heavy texture. It felt softer and smoother, and, as I was registering the change, I realized why the mermen didn't follow. The salt water was left behind; this was *fresh* water.

A sudden rush of this new, wonderful water pushed us through the cave faster than gas escapes the kraken. We shot forward so fast and hard that we scraped against the jagged edges (My poor suit!) and were thrown, surprisingly, out of the cave, outdoors, ten meters into open air, gasping. The rise turned into a fall, and we all landed hard on stone, having reached some sort of courtyard in the middle of Venus' castle.

(Light Techs, surely the audience members will be on the edge of their seat, overwrought. Raise the lights just a touch to ease the dizzying tension.)

All of us sucked in air. And hacked. And groaned. I heard the flap-flop of the mertail, which must have still had some life in it. I had known from the Orb of Diana that the cave didn't lead directly to Vulcan's underground trail, but I was nonetheless momentarily stunned at being on open land. I heard hurried footfalls and Tamara frantically asking Cupid if he was alright. His joy invaded my mind, and the feel of her arms around him enveloped me as well as she hugged and kissed him, clearly grateful that he was alright.

I chose to focus on the color-streaked sky above. The last of the sun must have dipped beyond the horizon. Tamara's face suddenly came into that view as well, her lovely dark eyes complementing the sunset sky behind her and asking if *I* was alright. No spider's web could compare to *her* concern. I nodded. It was all I had the strength for.

My panthers must have shaken themselves dry because drops of fresh water rained all around us. Pip stumbled into my leg and rested his nearly-drowned head on my thigh. *The impertinence!* I thought. And yet, here he was, nearly as drowned as the rest of us.

I was careful to not tip him as I sat up.

Chapter 12

PORTALS

C upid! What are you doing?!" Tamara cried.
I swiveled on my bottom to see Cupid frantically stripping down. He ripped off his grey shirt and threw it to the ground, creating a dark puddle at his feet. Then he grabbed hold of his pants waist and pushed it to his ankles, his ambrosia tray clanking to the ground along with his dignity. Cupid hoisted a leg free.

"Stop!" Tamara implored to no avail.

Cupid hopped in a circle on the liberated leg, trying to free the other one. His foot caught on the rumpled shirt, and he toppled sideways, the better to yank away the jumbled pants. In a half second, he was fully naked. He hotfooted to escape the offending attire.

(House Ushers, prepare for this from opening night on. The more prudish spectators may faint at the sight and slump out of their seats. Settle them back in. They'll rouse soon enough after the shock of it all.)

"WHY are you undressed?!" Tamara asked furiously.

Pip raised a weak hand to cover his eyes. I didn't bother. It was nothing I hadn't seen before.

"The clothes! Triton! Salt!"

Tamara didn't understand, and I wasn't about to clear things up lest I reveal my little privilege into Cupid's mind. That'd be a shame, so I let Cupid answer in his own way.

"Triton can move the salt in my clothes!" he gasped.

Tamara walked over to him and placed a conciliatory hand on his trembling shoulder.

"Sweetie, you're fine. You just seconds ago managed to launch everyone out of the cave – and rinse your clothes – because we just went through fresh water."

"And apparently very *c-o-o-o-o-o-ld* fresh water!" I crowed.

Pip let out a chuckle before slapping a hand to his mouth.

Cupid took a furious step toward me, but Tamara held his arm. "Go pick up your clothes and smell it. You'll see that it's fresh water, and you can rinse it some more in the well if you're worried about salt."

Cupid refrained from resorting to fisticuffs with me, which would be very amusing indeed because you just can't take a contender seriously if he's threatening in the buff. (Light Techs, cue the sickly yellow lighting.)

Cupid instead sidestepped Tamara and my cats, who had begun feasting on mertail, and stomped over to his soaked duds. He yanked them off the ground and fumbled furiously to pull them on.

(Note to Stage Producer: Lest we harm fragile minds in the audience, consider the venue. If this play be performed in a conservative town, perhaps our naked Cupid belongs backlit behind a screen. Come to think of it, if life were fair, this scene would have played out that way in real life.)

I'd had enough of Cupid's backside and so I looked ahead. Enclosing Venus' stone courtyard were giant boulders with curious openings, and beyond those, the purpling sky. I saw a shadow flit across my vision some hundred meters away.

"Sentinels!" I shout-whispered.

Cupid and Tamara, standing at that moment, immediately dropped to the ground. My cats flopped to their bellies, and everyone joined Pip and me in making ourselves shadows. Pip's whitish blue tint had turned solidly blue, but I could see him breathing. Perhaps he was just chilled.

Our whole group barely breathed, so sure we were that we'd be seen in that open space were anyone to merely look our way. Dusk was upon us, but lamplight was starting to become visible from the stone enclosures. They were rooms, I realized, and their light would give us away.

A second shadow joined the first and hovered. I couldn't tell, what with us in the light and they in the darkness, what they looked like. I couldn't even distinguish wings, and, knowing Vulcan's brilliance, any sentinels he'd create may very well not need them.

I turned my head slightly to ascertain everyone's position. I got an eyeful of ass instead. (Prop Master, two rotten honeydew melons placed side by side ought to just about portray it perfectly.) I looked away. Better my movement be seen, better to make eye contact with monstrous sentinels, than to face that sight again.

My movement didn't trigger an alarm, however. In fact, both sentinels, apparently having made a round and checked in, continued on their way. "They're gone," I whispered urgently. Pip lifted his head weakly.

"Saturn's stones!" Cupid cursed. "Why are we hiding? *I* can be here! This is my mom's house, remember?!"

Tamara got to her feet and looked his way. "But we aren't supposed to be here – on a secret mission. The good thing is those sentinels are looking for people coming *in*, not people already here. So we can keep going. Forward. There's no going back into that water."

Cupid's jaw clenched. He grabbed his drippy pants and pushed a leg in. "What is going on with Neptune's family anyway?!" he demanded. "What do they think I've *done* to them? I would never be so stupid as to offend them! Neptune's territory covers 70 percent of Earth. I can't do my job if I can't cross his domain! Bacchus!"

Cupid was apparently addressing me this whole time. Who knew?

"What have you got to say about this?" he demanded.

I used both hands to turn Pip's head and lay him gently on the tiles upon which we sat. I slowly stood and saw my cats wiggle back to the mertail and take a nibble. Placing a finger to my temple, I deliberately forced Cupid to wait. I pondered a moment. I'd heard no recent rumblings of sea embargoes, which occasionally happen when Neptune feels his territory's been disrespected. And the last time I'd seen Neptune was through the eyes of the nighttime wanderer who'd disturbed my dreams and inadvertently latched me to Cupid. I wondered if there was a connection. So, apparently, did Tamara.

"Bacchus," she asked, stepping up to me. Her features were softening in the fading evening light. "When you told us that Mercury had interrupted your dreams, you also said you'd later seen him talking to Neptune. Um, did Mercury ask Neptune to … maybe … fight Cupid?"

Aw, kraken crap, Cupid thought.

I laughed despite myself. "No, Tamara, he did not. Furthermore, had Neptune wanted to hurt or even kill Cupid, there's very little chance that he'd have failed -- not once but twice."

"Excuse me?" Cupid asked.

"Neptune commands the seas. He could have created a whirlpool just now, spun us to the sea floor, and released the maelstrom right on top of us. Easy peasy. No, if Neptune wished us to shuffle off this immortal coil, the only sea we'd later see would be the slim sea of The River Styx."

Cupid's attention snapped to Tamara. Her expression revealed nothing really, yet he stepped in front of me and warned, "Don't you mention The River Styx in front of her again."

Tamara bristled. "And don't you censor my conversations, Cupid."

That's the spirit! I thought, just a wee bit proud of myself for causing a stir, even if it was unintentional.

Pip coughed at my feet and began to stir with a bit more vigor. I watched him a moment to allow the lovebirds amongst us a chance to work things out, as of course they would. I noticed that he – and all seven of us – stood atop a sprawling mosaic of natural stone, each rock tiny, irregular, and richly hued. It would have taken mortals decades to gather so many beautiful stones and lay them in so elaborate a design. I wondered if they'd created it in their worship or if this particular mosaic was divinely devised.

It depicted a seaside kingdom, one that glowed more vibrantly with each passing moment. At the mosaic's bottom-most edge hid the unassuming natural spring from which *we* sprung. Its water blended perfectly with the mosaic's sparkling blue waves to hide the opening to the sea.

I moved my eyes up the tile masterpiece. The waves heaved and crashed onto a golden, sandy beach. I heard the water rush forward. I pictured myself stepping into that water, walking onto that beach, and losing myself in paradise's bliss. My eyes drifted past the beach. Black volcanic rock, splintered into rectangular prisms, jumbled together and created a landform upon which towered a white castle made of bleached sea foam. Walking bridges connected the fortress's many turrets, and from the graceful, arching bridges clung purple vines, hanging heavy with salmon pink roses. My eyes again drifted, downward, back toward the swaying sea. Brown tiles gathered together to form seahorses big enough for grown men to ride. The horses neighed and bounced along the waves. Pip was about to mount one.

"No, you idiot!" shouted Cupid, startling the two of us. He rushed over to yank Pip away from the tiles, like a monkey snatching a banana. Pip shouted something about riding the ponies. I shook my confused head and looked back at the mosaic. The seahorses stopped bouncing. Their hides splintered into innumerable brown tiles, their animation gone. The lovely blue tiles that formed the sea no longer swayed. The only sound of surf to be heard was that of the sea beyond the courtyard's rock walls, which was crashing against the rock rather more harshly than normal.

The mosaic's enchanted to beguile visitors, I realized,

late. My cats backed away, baring teeth.

"I bet the horse would have taken him straight to Venus, wherever she is, or to another mosaic near her," said Tamara.

"Or maybe it'd take a particularly pesky admirer back into the cave to be drowned," I assessed, solely to offend Cupid. I of course didn't mean it; Venus is all about love.

"My mother," pronounced Cupid with offense dripping from every syllable, "would never harm an admirer. Were she in the habit, she'd be doing nothing but harming people. Now Vulcan, well, that's another story."

I pondered his statement. Vulcan might well have created the mosaic as a trap, and his wayward wife may have cleverly added the spring later as her very own escape hatch. Fascinating.

Pip stared ahead, still caught in the mosaic's lulling enchantment, not offering the least bit of resistance to Cupid's continued grip around his waist.

"Nice save, sweetie," Tamara said, her tiff with her Truly apparently over. She looked to the skies again. "So where do you think Vulcan's trail might be?"

Cupid sighed and lowered his hands to his sides, thinking. Pip remained in Cupid's grip and so now hung sideways, his head and limbs drooping. A spray of seawater crashed into some rocks well beyond us and flew skyward. We were safe at this distance, but, my gods, I knew Triton was angry.

Cupid eyed the spray as it fell back to the sea and must have decided it best to move on. He looked around the courtyard. The room that I'd seen carved into a boulder was actually one of many rooms in many boulders that formed half-walls around the open space. The room was slowly brightening under the influence of enchanted lamplight, which spilled out onto the tiles. Cupid pointed at one room in particular.

It had been converted to a beauty salon, although I doubted that any of the mortal tourists who visit the palace would be able to see the beauty regalia ensconced within. The mortals who come here do so to be within arm's reach of history and also for the chance to kiss a partner in the fog that often rolls up the palace hill. Humans call the mist "Venus' Kiss," and, oh, how young lovers take advantage of it. No mortal would spot, as I did, the room's round brushes and old-fashioned beehive hair dryer, which reminded me of a mortal cliché: "The higher the hair, the closer to the gods."

(Stage Crew, raid the prop room from our production of Grease. No amount of silver hair foil could possibly be enough.)

Cupid kept looking around. Another room housed a hot tub and sauna. Next was a room with a massage table, oils, and dozens of torture-type devices that some might call muscle rollers. I wondered if Venus employed a masseur or a masseuse – and might you not fairly call one a massagonist or a massandrist? Ha! I was starting to get the impression that the goddess of beauty took her beauty regimen verrrrrrry seriously.

Cupid turned toward the other side of the court and spotted the only offshoot barred by a blackened, sooty, centuries-old, wooden door that looked to weigh about as much as the rest of the castle. How we didn't notice it right away amazed me – until I realized the mosaic's true purpose: to confound visitors to ignore the door, to let our eyes slide right past the wooden portal and return to the tiled fantasy. So it *was* Vulcan who'd enchanted the mosaic.

"That's got to be the way in," Tamara whispered.

"I believe you've charted our course, my treasure," I answered, ignoring that Cupid was actually the one who'd spotted the route. "The filth covering that door can only come from underground, from the ashy atmosphere of the land underfoot."

"I – I need – a second," croaked Pip, who was finally reviving enough to lift his head.

"We all will," I answered before turning to face my only other godly companion. "As you have no doubt surmised, Cupid, your mother would not deign to travel through the filth of the underground to meet her dreggy husband. Instead, she would surely fly through bright blue skies and softly scented breezes to arrive just as beautifully as when she left.

"Vulcan's Trail is meant for Vulcan's pleasure – and *his* alone. Its traps and trials will test our every skill. What secrets it hides only he knows – and its guilt pulses like The Tell-Tale Heart. Take a moment to gather your courage, everyone, and (I turned to Tamara) look at the beauty around you. We may never see the surface again."

(I'd like to thank the academy…)

Chapter 13

THE TOUCH

C upid reached behind his back and pulled his ambrosia tray from his waistband. It coughed up a half
dozen squares for each of us, and Cupid waved his hand
above it to reshape it into the form of cheese and crackers.
His courtesy did not go unnoticed nor did his wisdom to
power up before a trek, and so I too offered sustenance:
watered-down wine from my ever-filling goblet. Do not
laugh, mortal. As Cupid would surely concur, wine often
provides courage for acts both great and small, and water
prevents dehydration.

When we were all satiated and ready to begin,
Cupid raised his hand, palm up, along the outside edge
of the door. He paused at the mid-way point and smiled
before waving his hand side to side. A heavy thud on the
other side told us he'd knocked away the interior door latch.

"Hmmm," Cupid said before any of us could con-
gratulate him on a promising first success. "The door had
a wooden sliding latch, so it was easy for me to control
the wood's water to open it. But, it's strange. The latch is
meant to be opened or closed only from the inside."

"Well, Bacchus just said that Venus wouldn't go to
him through that cave," replied Tamara, "so the door didn't
need to open from the outside."

"But that also means that Vulcan would unlock the door to get here to the courtyard but couldn't close it behind him."

"Well," interjected Pip, "the god of fire surely felt secure that no one knowing his reputation would dare enter his cave. And, remember, mortals probably can't even see the door."

"But if someone did dare to enter the cave while Vulcan was in Venus' Castle..." Tamara spoke aloud.

"Vulcan could sneak in behind them and lock them in," I finished her sentence. "Then the trespasser would either have to face Vulcan or his traps. Either is a terrible choice."

I wish Tyrone, Tommy, Jarel, and Cornelius were here, Cupid thought. *They'd pump me up for this.*

I was taken aback by Cupid's admission, unspoken though it was. Here he had with him the love of his life (Tamara), me (a god who is no known coward), said god's fierce pets, and, well, Pip (and even that flyspeck messenger had to be of *some* use on this journey), yet Cupid panged for his former cast and crew. I suppose it *is* unsettling to face challenges with a new lineup, even for a god.

The sky above us disrobed its light purple and was quickly redressing in deepest blue. No time to lose. Pip must have thought the same because he fluttered to the door and pushed against it with all the might he could muster. It moved not an inch. Cupid again raised his hand toward the door and willed the water within to obey. The door groaned as if we had disturbed its peace and slowly swung open.

Despite the deepening darkness outside, our eyes had not yet grown accustomed to it, much less to the profound darkness that we encountered when we took our first steps inside. The blackness was impenetrable. The inky murk blurred the cave's stony walls along with the outlines of my accomplices, whom I knew to be beside me. Their figures became indiscernible, lost in the endlessness of black monotone. It was suddenly as if they ceased to exist, and I'd have bet my figgy pudding that this subterranean atmosphere was hexed specifically to inflict a sense of isolation.

More steps, and, with each, the darkness grew more oppressive. The air hung heavy with the settled soot of millennia. We all turned at once to check on the ancient, filthy door now a dozen paces behind us. It remained open yet allowed no light to pass its frame. I wished I hadn't left my thyrsus and its brightness at the bottom of the sea.

As one, we turned forward and took several more steps.

The gloom seemed infinite.

A few more hesitant steps.

The dark heaved under its own weight.

A single shuffle forward.

The blackness darkened.

"Whoa," Cupid muttered.

"Unfathomable," I replied.

"This – this is even darker than P-Pluto's fog," stammered Tamara. "I didn't know that was possible."

"You okay, TamTam?!" Cupid asked urgently and shuffled toward her. I heard a resounding crack followed by a howl. "Argh! My head! I hit something!"

The door swung closed behind us – much faster than it had opened. The latch self-locked with a thud.

"EEEEE!" someone squeaked.

A scuffle.

Crunching underfoot.

"Get off me!" Cupid bellowed.

"What's happening??!" Tamara demanded.

"Pip! Let go of me!"

"Sir, please! I can't see!" answered Pip.

"And I can't breathe with you wrapped around my neck!"

I smiled widely in unfettered glee. This was going even better than I'd hoped. Less than twenty paces into the cave and already the group was in disarray. Discord and drama were sure to follow.

"Stop, everyone! Just stop!" demanded Tamara.

I had in fact not moved an inch after speaking. I for one saw this coming and merely waited for the chaos to commence. I was eager to contribute to it. "Yes, everyone, hush! Let's all listen to Tamara. She seems to be the only one here keeping her wits about her."

Brown-noser! Cupid screamed in his head. *Instigator! Crrrreep!*

Let the undermining of the team begin.

"Bacchus,"Tamara continued. "Diana's Orb might be helpful."

"Ahhh, so it might!"I exclaimed, having thought of it some time ago but wanting to see how my companions might handle themselves first. I pulled off my backpack, withdrew the Orb, and extended it toward the darkness, like an offering. Its surface swirled brightly, yet its radiance only served to light itself; no light extended into the darkness. It appears that Vulcan had thought of everything.

"That thing'll only blind us from seeing enemies," Cupid muttered.

"En-enemies?" Pip quavered.

"Or predators," I added.

"Predators?!" Pip cried.

"Cut it out!" Cupid demanded. "Pip, loosen your grip!"

I had an inkling and lowered the Orb to our feet. My suspicions proved true. Diana's Orb just managed to cast a few shadows on the skulls and bones underfoot.

"WHAAAAA!" Pip screamed like a true Hollywood starlet.

Another scuffle. A tumble to the ground followed by a scramble to get back up.

"Pip! You're losing it!" Cupid shouted.

"Oh, he's well beyond having lost it," I corrected. "But he really ought to be quiet in here."

The scuffling immediately stopped, both Pip and Cupid breathing heavily.

"Let's just hold hands," Tamara suggested, "all of us, so we don't get separated."

There was a moment's hesitation, then furious movement as Cupid and I rushed to seize her hand. Alas, the lone lady had but two hands and she insisted on resting one on the shoulder of my alpha cat, whom she'd wisely suggested stand beside her.

That worm Cupid secured Tamara's other hand, and so he and I, after some uncomfortable squeamishness and hand wresting, grabbed hold of each other's sleeves. It was close enough to keep us all in a chain.

The cave narrowed and became too cramped to walk abreast, so our line bent to shuffle forward. After a dozen awkward paces, Cupid jerked his hand away.

"Did you feel that?" he asked.

My cats began a low snarl.

Indeed I had felt it, a tiny flutter on my skin, disquieting like the feeling of walking through a string of cobweb.

My cats shook themselves as if to dry. They growled.

"I-I-I-I felt something, too!" whined Pip in dismay.

I heard Cupid curse the little monkey in his head as Pip scrambled down his arm to reach Tamara's arm and presumably climb his way up to *her* neck.

"Pip!" she scolded.

"I'm sca--"

"Here it comes again!" Tamara warned.

The single flutter turned into many that were creeping their way up our arms, through our clothing, and becoming firmer, as if preparing to wrap us, to trap us. We broke our hands apart and brushed our arms. There was nothing there.

"What is this?" demanded Cupid.

"An irritant with snare potential," I offered helpfully.

This guy, I heard Cupid think.

"It's grabbing me!" interjected Pip.

"Hold on," demanded Tamara. "It's strangely... familiar. Pip, please loosen your grip. You're choking me."

"Loosen your grip, Pip, or *I'll choke you!*" threatened Cupid.

Pip squeaked, and Tamara shuffled forward without us.

"Tamara, don't!" shouted Cupid – but too late. She stepped out of his reach. Upon her first steps, the gossamer strands touched our skins once more and began flittering their way around us. In a fraction of a second, their weightlessness mutated to the heft of hundred-pound ropes. They fell upon us, collapsing like the 50-foot-tall, red velvet curtains that drape the stages of the oldest, finest theatres – only, this fabric, these strange tendrils, intended to pin us in the cave for all eternity. Pip was crying.

Tamara's footfalls stopped. She breathed heavily, as if a boa constrictor were squeezing her lungs, loving her, its prey, to death.

"It's… it's like Pluto's fog, don't you see?" Tamara said, effort in her every syllable. "It doesn't create dread, exactly, like the fog did, but the faster we move and the more unnerved we are, the more they want to trap us, the more their darkness wants to crush us. Discourage us. Make us want to lie down and die." She cleared her throat and, when she next spoke, sounded stronger. "Pip's panic is making it worse for him. He's writhing like crazy – stop it, Pip!" I heard a squeak and got the distinct impression that she'd grabbed hold of him to physically restrain him. "Look, we've stopped moving and the strands aren't after us again. They're touching me but they're not enveloping me. I think we need to walk forward without panic. Pip, do you hear me? Control yourself so we can move forward."

I was sure that, if I could see Cupid's face, I'd see absolute panic in its purest form at the thought of moving forward into that trap with his beloved.

"Be brave," she commanded Pip. He must have stilled because his whimpering silenced. I, along with the entire celestial world, had heard of Tamara's fearlessness, but to see it in action was inspiring – and ensnaring on its own.

"Grab hands again, and I'll lead," Tamara commanded.

"Say what?!" demanded Cupid.

"I've done this before, Cupid. I can handle these mind games. Bacchus?"

"Yes, my darling?" I answered in another Freudian slip.

Cupid's onslaught of unspoken oaths were quite threatening indeed. His hostility was palpable. My panthers rumbled in warning.

Tamara must have reached out to the panther nearest her because it quieted. We, like it, heeded her and tethered ourselves to each other for the slow trek through the black, uncharted cave. The two remaining pards positioned themselves at rear.

I heard Cupid think in rapid fire of a hundred reasons why she shouldn't lead, but we were already walking, descending further into the Earth with each step, and Tamara's slow, unwavering pace kept the threads at bay.

"Steady," she would occasionally reassure us. It was always needed. As much as my godly cool and wine-numbed mind can let much trouble slide off, the heavy blackness and fingerlike grazes regularly brought us to the edge of panic – or hopelessness -- or hypnotic drowsiness.

(Maestro, lead the orchestra through a deep, thrumming, repetitive pulse. You'll want to lull the theatre-goers into quiet submission.)

Cupid, in a moment of carelessness, let down his guard. The tendrils enveloped him. He imagined – and thus I saw in my mind – the drowning waters of the sea just beyond these cave walls. Cupid surrendered to them, almost welcoming death, caressing as it was. The tendrils lulled him, obliterating his resistance to their black danger, and I along with him, likely due to our mental connection. He was very near to succumbing, and truth demands that I admit the same for me.

"One foot ahead of the other," Tamara urged.

Cupid stopped altogether.

"Concentrate on the end of this tunnel," Tamara coached, pulling us all along.

Her voice broke into my mind. I pushed Cupid hard. He stumbled toward the cave's walls.

"Cupid," Tamara said, clearly feeling his hand pull away from her. She stopped a moment and prodded, "Soothe your thoughts. Keep walking."

Her control radiated out to the rest of us. Even my cats, silent as the swallowing blackness around them, occasionally brushed against our hands, nudging us, spurred by Tamara's words.

"Be calm, Pip."

Her words snapped Cupid out of his doldrums. I felt Cupid's urge to pull Pip away, but he decided that fast moves weren't advisable just then. We kept walking. It felt like forever. And then forever again.

Eventually, finally, we heard her hum, "There's light ahead," and indeed we saw a faraway doorway with light escaping its edges. "Don't run," she urged, mere fractions of a second before we revved to do so. A collective sigh preceded the grueling, closing fifty paces. The final stretch was punctuated by the crunching of the especially thick carpet of skulls and bones concentrated here.

As soon as we reached the door, both the blackness and the panic ebbed. We bathed in the shallow light, and I watched Tamara smile at herself and Pip rub his brow in shame. Cupid looked drained from worry.

It would be best to consider this first challenge the easy part. We took a moment to collect ourselves, and then I turned the door's cool, glass knob, subjecting us to what lay beyond.

Chapter 14

THE LEDGE AND THE HEDGE

I opened the door to a bright, round room. Its white marble floor looked smooth as fondant icing and spread to touch glassy, light yellow walls. The walls rose to a substantial height, at least three stories, before sloping inward to create a domed ceiling. At the dome's peak hung a giant, sparkling diamond chandelier that reflected the light of a dozen inconsumable candles suspended within a round candelabra. The chandelier was real diamond, I was convinced. Vulcan, the god of metallurgy, would surely come across a few diamonds on his travels, enough even to piece together this splendid lodestar. Of course, Vulcan could also create diamonds at will in the palm of his hand, much as how mortals shape snowballs, applying incredible pressure to a lump of carbon and blowing on it throughout.

"This room's for my mom," Cupid said almost too quietly to be heard. But I nodded to him in agreement. The impressive chandelier, the lightly colored walls with two elegant little ledges spiraling downward like a double helix to the pale floor immediately told me, too, that Vulcan made this room as a restful rendezvous. My panthers inhaled deeply, their eyelids drooped peacefully.

"But," whispered Pip, one arm still wrapped around Tamara's neck and the other continuing to rub his brow.

He stopped to point back through the door. "She'd have to go through that horrible darkness to get here. And she wouldn't want to be underground. We decided that."

"And there's no furniture," added Tamara. "Although maybe there once was. Pip, please." She must have decided that Pip was safe enough here to peel him from her neck. It was not unlike ripping off a bandage. He resisted at first, but his dignity must have gotten the better of him; he fluttered his buggy wings to hover at eye level.

(Stagehands, portray Pip as a blue and white striped, lumpy beanbag dangling from a string. Shake the line often to show him quiver.)

"It's odd, don't you think?" pondered Tamara aloud. "Why would Vulcan keep up a room for Venus knowing that she probably won't visit, that's nearly impossible to get to, and that has no furniture and no place to sit or have a drink?"

We all paused.

"I don't buy it."

No sooner were her words spoken than the door from whence we came swung shut and blended into its glass wall. Cupid lunged. The moment his palm touched the phantom door, mechanical whirring broke all around.

We jolted. My cats growled. The whirring sound grew, and we looked around for its source. Within it came the lone ring of a single bell, sharp and distinct. The single t-i-i-i-i-ing resonated and was soon joined by another ten, amplified by a hundred, overwhelmed by more. The deafening tintinnabulation would have made even the Singing Sirens cover their ears.

"Bacchus, what's happening?!" demanded Cupid. He pulled his bow forward and teed up an arrow.

Before I could take a guess sure to be as good as anyone else's, Pip squealed and dived back toward Tamara. He plastered himself around her neck just as we saw the beginnings of the onslaught.

Above us, at the base of the dome and at the very top of each thin ledge, an opening came to light, not noticeable at first, but from which now spilled several blue and purple crystals, each between two and four inches long. They didn't rest at the top of the ledge as if pushed there by someone on the other side of the opening; instead, they shuddered and quaked and shimmied until they finally popped like corn kernels. Only, this wasn't entertaining like popcorn. The gems erupted crystalline shoots, jutting out from their centers to create jointy legs.

The gems that came out on either side of the room lifted themselves on their spindly, lithic legs and made way for others behind them. These newly mobile rocks scuttled and slid their way down the ledge, and it quickly became clear to all of us that the shallow ledge's singular purpose was to allow their advance.

"Bacchus?!" asked Cupid, swiveling his ready bow

toward the curios. As I hadn't had the chance earlier to answer that I had no more experience battling Vulcan's contrivances than he, I suppose he really did believe me capable of a suggestion. I had none but was sure that we as gods could figure it out.

I looked up to see dozens more of the craggy creatures spilling out on the ledge and scuttling down. **(Stagehands, suggest the multitude by lowering a disco ball just out of sight and casting its flecks of light all around.)**

The gems were nearly upon us. My wildcats roared in warning.

"I suggest we ready our defenses," I advised.

Useless! I heard Cupid think. Again, his conclusion was unfair. It was a perfectly useful suggestion and one that, I might add, he immediately followed. Cupid stepped in front of Tamara right as the first adamant attacked. It leapt off the glassy ledge just as Cupid fired. The gem was thrown off course, but another landed with startling precision onto Cupid's arm. Before Cupid could shake it off, it sank a limb-like propulsion into his exposed flesh and dragged the chiseled blade up his arm, filleting him.

"Waaaaah!" Cupid howled and spun so quickly that both the crystal critter and Tamara were thrown back. Tamara landed at the base of one of the ledges and was immediately set upon by crystals.

"Tamara!" Cupid wailed and lunged toward her. The dozens of crystals already upon her bounced from that beautiful port to land on him.

I'd never make that mistake.

Each buried a bit of themselves into Cupid's flesh and set off even more howling and splattering of godly blood. The two subordinate panthers surrounded me and slapped the minerals out of plain air; the alpha panther shielded Tamara. I was proud of him for discerning who was important, but it turned out not to be needed.

"The gemstones aren't attacking Tamara!" I called to Cupid, who may not have heard me over his own shouting.

"Or Pip or the panthers!" shouted Tamara, leaping to her feet. "Maybe Vulcan thinks men are his only threat, that women won't try to seduce Venus."

"Have you *seen* the way some women look at my mother?!" Cupid bellowed while jerking his arms wildly.

A larger batch of animated crystals rained down from above, several landing on my arms, cutting into me as well. My wails joined Cupid's.

"Bacchus!" Cupid shouted, ripping the not-so-charming little sparklers off of himself.

"Yes, I know what to do!" I answered, being a god and able to abate a few problems at least. I spun to remove the daggering varmints lest my tattoos spring to life, which would be even more painful, believe it or not. I called out, "Vines!" and dropped my backpack.

Another crystal landed on my back and slashed through my suit coat. Before I could shake it away, an arrow lanced it and sent it careening into the glass wall. My breath caught as I realized the arrow flew within a millimeter of my very spine. I turned to berate Cupid but instead spotted Tamara, standing, legs splayed in balance, bow and arrow poised, a look of intense concentration in her eyes as she shot crystals out of mid-air. What bearing. What bravery and mien. The magnificent champion.

I returned to my backpack, dug out my ambrosia tray, and joined her in battering the little leaping beasties. My cats gleefully did the same, but we were vastly outnumbered.

"The vines need time to get here!" I called to Cupid. "Use your water!"

Swinging his blood-soaked arms in as graceful an arc as I had done with my thyrsus – and don't you dare tell me that he didn't learn that from me – Cupid conjured a spinning water ball around us two. He rolled his hands – and thus the water – with enough force to repel the jumping jewels. It couldn't last forever, even though the beasties' attack likely would.

Tamara jumped up and grabbed hold of the ledge, presumably to climb to its apex, but the ledge was too shallow and smooth to allow a firm grip. She landed hard on the marble floor and mouthed something in our direction. We couldn't hear over the rushing water and clanging bells, yet we recognize a lost cause.

"What now?!" shouted Cupid over the roaring whorl.

"I'll get crybaby over there involved!" I held my breath for the surge and leapt out of the watery mass. Crystals beset me, and a few managed to slip into the sphere through the hole I'd just made. Cupid and I yowled in unison, but a sacrifice had to be made, and by the gods if I wasn't happy to make it.

I lunged at Tamara, ripped Pip off her neck, and threw him like a baseball toward the dome. Then, ripping more crystals off my arm – and spilling my ichor with them, mind you – I shouted, "Get in one of those holes and turn off whatever's triggering them! Look for the bells!"

Tamara never stopped firing, clearing the path for him.

I too needed shelter. I turned back toward the water sphere at the moment it collapsed and Cupid fell to the ground. He couldn't simultaneously rip the crystals off him and keep the waters moving. He was losing blood. One of my panthers pounced on him. Cupid screamed, and through our mental connection I saw his vision of being eaten alive by a wildcat. I chuckled as the cat ignored him and batted away gemstones.

My vines arrived just as Cupid's screams died.

The walls around us shook and cracked. Every vine of every type within 10 miles burrowed under my deific demand and drilled through the glassy finish of the walls. When they broke through, they reached out to ensnare every crystal they touched. We watched the ever-morphing flurry of slithering vines wrapping up gemstones, themselves twitching and jerking. It looked like the very walls were wearing countless, living jeweled necklaces, all struggling to escape. What a marvelous sight.

Cupid watched as the gemmy wonders cut their way free but were immediately recaptured by my relentless vines, either the same vine reconstituting itself or a fresh vine come to relieve its brother. This stopgap wouldn't last. And the exertion of blindly summoning vines without my thyrsus to pinpoint them had taken its toll on me.

I looked up to see Pip still quavering aloft, frozen in fear. He hadn't moved. "Now! Go!" I commanded. He ignored me.

"Pip, move!" Tamara shouted.

It appeared that her orders were to be obeyed. Pip fluttered closer to the opening from whence the critters came but stopped to whimper. He turned solidly yellow. I was sorely tempted to have a vine strangle him.

"Be brave, Pip!"

He looked down at her and openly bawled.

"We need you!"

The pandering words finally prompted Pip's pluck – or his pride. He breathed deeply before swooping into the tiny cranny, no bigger than a mouse hole, and crawling in.

The bound gems switched to a different tactic. Rather than extending crystals to make limbs or to cut through the vines, they instead began firing them like tiny daggers. The cats fell back; they couldn't stop that many spears. Cupid had lost too much blood to conjure more watery protection, so I held my ambrosia tray like a shield over us.

Tamara turned her bow toward us. Her arrows knocked the projectiles out of the open air. She was outstanding while we awaited help from that bratty housefly of ours. I heard Pip scream and cry and Tamara call out encouragement. And suddenly the bells stopped tinging, and the crystal daggers stopped thudding against my tray, and a clamor of gemstones rained down onto the marble floor and spilled across the tiles and spun to a stop. And then there was blessed silence.

Except for the next sound: Pip's whooping as he swooped out of the cavity, twittering about how he'd really done it, how he'd found the trigger and pulled the lever and stopped the attack and how about that?

It was no fun looking at Cupid and realizing that Pip, that Cowardly Lion, had just saved us from perishing in Oz.

Chapter 15

DINNER AND A SHOW

Pip became insufferable over the next several hours, which we spent in triage in the treasure room, as I chose to call it, as there was a king's ransom in jewels on the ground. Even King Midas would have been satisfied.

"The walls in that hole were dreadfully jagged," Pip said, spinning his heroic yarn. "And I was quite sure that I'd meet with more gems further in, trying to make their way out, but I was brave, like Tamara said. See this rip down my leg where a sharp edge caught me?" He pointed to a tiny red mark possibly half an inch long.

"But I kept going, climbing over hills and valleys. It was dark, so I had to keep my hands on the walls until I finally touched metal. I heard your shouts outside, and I couldn't have my army hurt-"

"*Your* army?" Cupid muttered weakly.

Pip ignored him. "-and so I grabbed and shook every piece of metal I could find. The first was the bell. Imagine my surprise when I moved it and the clapper rang louder. I know I heard more of those killer crystals break away behind me."

That little fart actually intensified the attack, Cupid realized.

"But I couldn't worry about that-"

"I bet," accused Cupid.

"My crew was depending on me."

Your crew?!

"And so I climbed over and under every bit of machinery I could find. You all are ve-e-e-e-e-e-ry lucky to have had me here because there would have been no way whatsoever that you could have reached that machinery to stop the attack."

I could have bore you like a shield and let the gems slice you rather than me, thought Cupid.

It was not a bad idea.

Tamara listened to the exchange patiently.

"And then things got reeeeeally dangerous," the speck said, growing neon pink as his tale revved up.

"Heaven's constellations!" I cried. "With all that trial and tribulation, I'm sure you fancy a snack." I pulled out my tray, both to put enough food into Pip's mouth to shut him up and also to help Cupid recover from his serious blood loss. I, *bon vivant*, oenophile, and gastronome that I am, conjured an absolute extravaganza of ambrosia and transformed the heavenly treats into *amuse-gueule*, arugula salads with nut sides, seafood mains, leavened breads, and a great many mousse desserts. And of course I brought forth my ever-filling wine goblet. I commanded my vanquishing vines to discharge a final duty before dismissal: to weave themselves tightly into eloquent wine glasses for the others, into which I poured my richest gift.

Eating alfresco and seated on the open ground is my norm, as it is for my cats. However, after Cupid offered his tray as a plate for Tamara, my alpha cat behaved most unusually and lay down before her to offer his back as her table. I hoped that my constant concern for those around me (my audience) is what inspired his odd courtesy.

Pip managed to show not an ounce of concern for *his* audience, gloating non-stop about his victory and, mouth full, regaling us not only with spittle but even more blow-by-blow minutia of the dangers he faced within the mouse hole, which I imagined to be slight indeed, at least less dire than he contended. I considered again dispatching a vine to dispatch *him*, but Tamara maintained a kind attentiveness which I was powerless to disturb.

To numb the pain of Pip's voice, I contemplated the fate of any mortals careless enough to stumble into Vulcan's cave, unlikely though that would be. Had they somehow made it past the creepy-crawly, mind-warping antechamber to reach this treasure room, they'd never reach beyond, not only because they'd likely get sliced to bits, but because, even if they did manage to defeat the beheading baubles, the mortals would likely try to gather the treasures and go back the way they'd come. I imagined how unforgiving the cave would be after a loss. I knew then that we could never retrace our steps.

"Pip, I need rest," Cupid uttered. "Would you please stop yammering?"

I realized that I'd been so busy ignoring Pip that I wasn't listening to Cupid's thoughts, but this finally was a thought worth hearing. Pip gaped. I found myself in Cupid's corner.

"We're fed and watered," I assessed, "and considering that we entered the cave at dusk, it's probably nearly morning already. Now we rest. In quiet."

Cupid, lying on his back, brought up his arm for a pillow. Tamara removed Cupid's tray from my alpha's back and ran a hand from its neck to its hip, both to remove any crumbs and possibly as a gentle thanks. I marveled at her fearlessness with my panthers. She then topped herself in my estimation by gently tipping the alpha on its side toward her, whispering something to it, and then lying perpendicular to it so as to rest her head on its shoulder.

My cat never protested, and I fell asleep to the unusual sound of purring.

I woke first, as dipsomaniacs are also often insomniacs.

The room continued to gleam a gentle yellow. The crystals remained motionless on the marble floor. No bells chimed. Pip muttered between his snores. "Yes, we're here." Zzzzz. "We'll have it soon." Zzzzz. "I hope." Zzzzz.

I tapped his foot with my own. "Tell him to go screw himself."

"M'kay. Zzzzz. Go screw yourself. Zzzzz."

I nodded and turned my attention to Cupid's wounds. They'd healed, and I knew he'd wake soon, his manly nature demanding alertness to danger. I rolled up my sleeves and saw no major wounds to the ivy tattoos on my wrist. They noticed my attention, slithered, and waved. I looked up before they'd become even more animated, setting my eyes on Tamara. She slumbered peacefully with an arm draped over my cat's ribs. I imagined she had slept the same against Cerberus at one time or another – and Cupid, that inexplicably lucky louse.

Tamara stirred, and I looked away lest she catch me staring, which I realized I was rudely doing.

"Bacchus?" she whispered.

I returned my gaze.

"Nice tats," she said sleepily.

I looked at them for the millionth time: inky black vines, dark green leaves, stemming from my wrists and climbing to mid-forearm. I looked back toward Tamara, who was watching them intently.

"They're moving," she marveled.

"Perhaps they're saying hello," I nearly hummed.

She chose not to take the bait. "What do you think is next?"

"The worst yet," I answered simply, hoping that

later she might notice more of me than my wrists. "This cave is hidden from Diana's Orb, as anyone would suspect it would be, but I imagine we're nearly there, and so the threat is greatest."

"Bacchus," Cupid grumbled.

'Yes, it's time to go,'' I replied, accidentally answering his unspoken question.

Cupid cocked his head suspiciously.

I casually rolled my sleeves back down. "You've healed, and our time is fleeting."

Pip lifted his head from the base of the ledge, where he'd settled "for our personal protection" should the gems reanimate. I never felt safer, you can imagine.

The celestials rose, the panthers stretched, and I tucked my suit coat into my backpack and walked to the side of the room opposite where we'd entered. Patting the walls, I discovered a well camouflaged doorknob, the only sign of a door cut so snugly out of its wall that nary a leaf of paper could slip between.

"Wait. Shouldn't I lead?" asked Pip, the popinjay.

"Oh, by all means!" I crowed before Cupid had a chance to berate the little gasbag. "Just as Hercules wrestled and defeated the Nemean lion, so you have defeated the Cleavers of Crystal Cave. It is fitting that you lead."

Pip dived for the doorknob and pulled. It didn't budge. He tried again, straining and grunting. Nothing. "If someone would just open the door," Pip petitioned, "I could forge ahead."

And be the first to get eaten, thought Cupid.

I felt that he really should have said that out loud. But that might prevent the comedy altogether.

Cupid shooed Pip away, opened the door effortlessly, and walked on through.

Chapter 16

THE GIRL IS MINE

What greeted him – and us – when we passed through the door's threshold can only be described as utter radiance.

A tubular passageway stretched out before us, ten meters around and achingly beautiful. Its blue-green walls glowed, phosphorescent. Light swayed along its surface as if bouncing off ocean waves. An intriguing, iridescent groove corkscrewed around and down the wall, disappearing into the distance. The whole thing looked as if Vulcan had churned a gigantic drill through the rock and left in its wake this glowing sea of a tunnel with an elegant, lustrous ribbon as a remnant.

This is even more my mother's style, thought Cupid, *but I'm not fallin' for that crap again.*

"Beautiful," Tamara whispered.

Cupid placed a possessive arm around her shoulder and drew her to him. "But probably deadly. Don't let it relax you, ma chère." He caressed her chin between thumb and forefinger. "I'm sure that's its purpose. And please know that your beauty far surpasses the meager glow of this dull stone."

I refrained from laughing. Camp is not theatre, as the boy apparently has yet to learn. Even so, the lovers drew closer, and so I averted my sullen eyes.

As I gave them privacy, I caught a tiny movement that I first thought to be the cave's swaying light playing on the sleek, black backs of my gorgeous panthers. But no. The cats themselves moved, quiet and fluid.

I suppose that it's only my many years in their company that's taught me their subtle mannerisms. I noticed them tilt their heads no more than an inch and drop their eyes toward our feet. There was nothing there except a nearly imperceptible line of ash running straight down the centerline of our path, disappearing into the distance. The ash might have simply settled, like silt on a river bed.

I looked back at Cupid and Tamara, who were leaning against the far side of the tunnel, breaking off a kiss. Pip pounced on their free moment to begin anew his constant peeping. Peep, peep, peep, like a demanding baby bird: I'm so brave. I'm so wonderful. Pay attention to me. Blah, blah, blah.

(Stagehands, I know that by now you'd love to take that bean bag Pip you suspended earlier and bash it like a piñata, but give it one more good quiver and then set the spotlight on me. You won't want to miss my next move.)

My cats separated. The two subordinates inched their way toward Cupid. The alpha stood in the middle with me, straddling the ashy line. He growled softly.

I turned to face him openly. He flicked his eyes up at me, then at Tamara, and bounded toward my wall. In the fractions of a second remaining, I grabbed Tamara's forearm and pulled her over the line – and into my arms.

What the-? thought Cupid, his arms still outreached.

I winked at him, his jaw dropped, and a wall of lava burst up from the ash between us.

"Aaaaaaaaagh!" screamed Pip. "Vulcan's found us! Whaaaaa!" He zipped in zigzags, screaming in hysterics. I delighted in seeing him, through the molten rock, dive at Cupid and wrap himself around his neck. Cupid grabbed hold of Pip's middle and pulled like a mortal might peel off a leech.

The blazing fire sealed the door from whence we came, and suddenly thickened so that we could no longer see each other on far sides of the tunnel. We could thank Vulcan's vagary that the fire did not burn hot.

"Tamara!" Cupid bellowed. "Pip! Get off me! Tamara, are you alright?"

Thus Cupid showed the fickle nature of Love: devotedness to one teammate and impatience toward the other. Gods and their hypocrisies.

"Cupid!" Tamara shouted through the lava wall. "I'm fine! Are you okay?!"

"Except for this tick attached to my neck! Bacchus!"

"Yes, my friend?"

"Don't you 'friend' me, you hydra in the grass! You saw this coming and stole my girl!"

The recipient of his affection looked up at me with a raised brow, awaiting my justification. The wall flared menacingly, and my alpha growled again.

"Why, Cupid, I'm offended," I said to both him and her. (I was not at all offended but instead entirely amused.) "I merely sensed danger and brought her into the care of my alpha, with whom she's developed a bond. I was looking out for her alone."

"I want her back!" he demanded.

"And of course you'll have her, should she wish it. It is never up to anyone but her." I was earning brownie points with every word spoken.

Suddenly my panthers roared in urgency. The alpha slammed into our legs to move us forward, and I could tell by Cupid's yelp that the others did the same. We'd taken not five paces before the lava wall bent in behind us. Suddenly we were walled on two sides by lava and the other sides by stone. The only way to go was straight ahead, and the progressing lava demanded our immediate advance.

"I cannot deliver Tamara," I told Cupid. "But, as The Bard advises, think not too closely on the event! There is a tide in the affairs of men. Perhaps our tide is to see each other at the end. Until then, I will treat Tamara as if she were my own."

"Don't you dare!" he retorted. The rest of his thoughts I cannot, as a gentleman, detail.

DIVIDE AND CONQUER

Set Designers, as this scene is divided in halves, my side of the tube and Cupid's side, you will need to construct a division center stage, a thin slit running from the backdrop right up to the orchestra pit, through which you'll raise the sheerest fabrics of reds, oranges, and yellows. Beneath them place blowing fans; the billowing fabrics will mimic the roiling lava wall separating our two factions. You'll also need two much smaller curtains of the same fabrics on a rolling base, positioned perpendicularly to the large lava wall; the curtains will follow the actors and panthers as they slowly advance toward the audience. The panthers will be human extras in black velvet. Bathe the remaining stage in swirling, blue-green lighting to mimic the passageway's phosphorescence.)

(My dear reader, I switch now to play script to best present the two sides, as the hissing lava wall prevents any direct communication between our groups. I continue to hear Cupid's unspoken thoughts, shown here in italics and voiced offstage. Cupid's spoken words are shown in plain text and spoken aloud by the actor on stage. The only character absent of dialogue is Pip (thank the gods), as I cannot hear Pip's voice through Cupid's thoughts. When I assume Pip speaks, a stagehand positioned stage left in dress blacks will express his dialogue as the single ting of a golden bell. A ting is actually the only sound that Pip, that petulant – or should I say PESTulant – tormentor, should ever make. And so we resume...)

CUPID: Pip, I swear, if you don't get off my neck, I'll rip you off myself and purposely hurl you into the lava.

TING

CUPID: I don't care. And keep moving or the fire's gonna fry our butts.

TING

CUPID: No, I don't have any control over them! They're Bacchus' panthers! I'm sure they're just waiting for us to stumble into the lava so they can have themselves a barbecue. Wha-! Arrrrghhh! Pip, get offa me!

TAMARA (places both hands on my arm as we plod, the lava behind us advancing even as the lava wall beside us roils): Bacchus, what is the point of this-this- separation?

ME (smiling like the panther that ate the canary): I imagine it's to see if a team divided possesses enough shared skills to survive.

TAMARA (raising a worried eyebrow): But what if the team is split unevenly?

ME (lowering my head toward her in most dramatic fashion): I believe Vulcan is counting on that.

TAMARA (closes her eyes for several moments): I'm worried, Bacchus. Aside from Vulcan's challenges, how will we steal his crown?

ME: We? *We* are accompanying Cupid on his mission, but he is the one commanded to steal. (raising both hands to Tamara's immediate protest) Pip was emphatic that Cupid steal the crown. Perhaps Jupiter has a specific reason for that.

CUPID: *That lush. That boozing bozo of a god. That thief. Aren't I supposed to be the thief here? How did Bacchus manage to get Tamara right out of my arms?!*

ME (laughing)

TAMARA (stops walking): You think it's funny that Cupid's on the hook here?

ALPHA (snarls and bumps into my leg)

ME (shaking my head in denial): Of course it's not funny, but keep walking, my dear. My alpha valiantly protects us by walking between us and the advancing lava, but let's not shorten the distance between him and molten earth.

TAMARA (resumes walking, looks over her shoulder): I'm sorry, uh. (turning back to me) Bacchus, what's his name?

ME (raising my chin): One does not name animals one wishes to remain wild.

TAMARA: He's not wild. He helps you and guides you. He's a guide cat.

ME (laughing): Even mortals know that such a thing

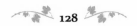

will never exist.

CUPID: *That snide jerk. I bet right now he's trying to smooth talk her.*

TAMARA (frowning): Animals can be trained.

ME (smiling to lighten the mood): Wise words from a wise woman. You are of course correct, Tamara, but trained animals tend to trust the species of their master, and I'd rather have my cats on alert with all beings, as is their nature, and ready to act without my approval.

TAMARA (pouts her lips in thought): I suppose I can see your point. Your panthers mean a great deal to you. I respect that.

CUPID: *At least she'll never respect him. She's smart enough to figure out what a phony he is.* WHAT, Pip?! What are you going on about?!

TING

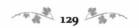

TING
TING
TING

TAMARA (shaking my arm): Bacchus, what's wrong with you?

ME (A vision from Cupid's mind bursts through my thoughts. Dozens of strings of lava shoot out from the lava wall toward the tunnel's curved outer edges. The fiery rays crisscross to block our path and in so doing create a laser maze through which not even the most agile human spy could contort.) **(Stagehands, recreate this by sneaking onstage in dress blacks and zinging Chinese yo-yos across our path. Keep the coil extended. The paper of the yo-yo may be red, orange, or yellow.)** (Cupid stutter-stops but is bumped from behind; he looks back toward the panthers and the lava behind. He can't stop lest he be burned to bits – barbecued, as he'd foreseen.): The final challenge.
(The fiery spears shoot across our path as well.)

TAMARA (shouts and tightens her grip on my arm, to my delight): Bacchus! It's trapping us!

ME (turning to look into her deep, dark eyes): Never fear, my dear. I will get us through this. (places fingers to temples in a show of concentration while waiting for Cupid to figure out how we'll get through this; my conduit's mind is firing a thousand thoughts a second. The panthers roar and swat at our legs for us to move.)

CUPID (nearing the first braided chord of fire.): Wait! Do you see that, Pip?!

TING

CUPID: Get your face out of my neck long enough to stare death in the face, you gutless gremlin!

ME (gasps loudly; could Cupid finally be exhibiting the patrimony of his warlord father, Mars?)

TAMARA: What, Bacchus? Have you figured it out?

ME (nods): I believe so, my dear. (waits for Cupid to prove my words true)

TING

CUPID: Now *I'm* talking! Look at the lava wall! It opens a tiny hole before it fires, like it's breathing in lava to blow it out hard.

ME (sees in Cupid's mind both his plan of attack and the drawing of his first arrow.): We attack the wall, Love.

TAMARA (steeples her brow): We what?!

ME (swiveling my backpack forward and dislodging my ambrosia tray even as Cupid shoots his first arrow. The peephole closes before his arrow hits the mark; his wooden lance bursts into flames.) (Prop Master, supply the Cupid actor with foam arrows that stop at the billowing curtain and slip below stage. We, unlike Gallagher, cannot risk spraying our audience with projectiles. Fruit smashing has its place, of course, so long as it excludes grapes, for such brutality could never produce good wine.):
We attack the wall before it attacks us.

CUPID (continues firing, each arrow becoming a blackened mass of ash at the wall's base): Pip, you need to get off me and get to the lava. Hover in front of a hole when you see it opening so I can fire at you.

TING

CUPID: Yes, exactly like William Tell's son!

ME (sniffing, smelling singed wings) **(Stagehands, fry some bacon offstage and waft it toward the groundlings.)**

CUPID (waving his drawn arrow): Pip, don't get too close! That lava beam isn't silly string! Hover in front of it and then move the second you see me draw back the bowstring! I'll have aimed by then.

ME **(Stagehands, swing the beanbag Pip as**

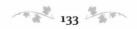

if it were a lantern caught in a storm at sea. This should be vigorous enough to require regular beanbag re-stitching. Be careful not to tangle him with the yo-yos or the bell-ringer onstage. Let's not repeat the fiasco of our opening night of Hamlet.) (My dear reader, let me tell you, that was a bad opener. The star got overexcited, swung the "poisoned" sword everywhere, and "killed off" every player. It turned a classic tragedy into a most unexpected comedy.) (Back to the scene playing before us, I wave a hand over my ambrosia tray, transform the ambrosia squares into champagne bottles, and hand the tray to Tamara. I grab a bottle and shake it vigorously.):

Tamara, please be my eyes and tell me when you see a hole forming in the wall.

TING

CUPID (drawing): Move!

TAMARA (points to a burgeoning breach): There!

ME (flicking my practiced fingers under the ridge of the

champagne bottle's bulbous cork; the cork fires like a rocket toward the hole; the frothy champagne hisses as it hits lava.)

CUPID (whooping as his arrow flies through the fissure, even though I'd half expected him to cheer more had the arrow struck Pip. The gap closes, its energy blown, no lava launched.): Yes!!! Panthers, move up! (The panthers on his side of the tunnel roar and slash the outer wall.)

ME (whooping as my champagne cork pierces the puncture): Yes!!! (smiling at Tamara's wide eyes) How many years do you imagine that I've played darts in bars, my sweet Tamara? Now we move up! (My alpha roars and sprays its smooth wall, marking an obvious victory.) **(Stage-hands, show this with a squirt from a hose discreetly hidden for the purpose.)** (I laugh – better here than my penthouse, and yet another reason to keep cats wild.)

TING

CUPID: Aaaand… move!

TAMARA: There!

ME (snagging another champagne bottle and showing off a bit with a low shot): Aaaand… move!

ME (smelling more burnt buggy wings) (Stagehands, more bacon. Order's up!)

TING

CUPID: I can't help that they're close. You just get ahead of them! (steps back and tramples a cat's paw; it attacks his ankle) Yeeeeeah! Stop it! Stop, you stupid creature! Why are you biting *me*? (the cat snarls) If you don't like it there, move ahead, both of you! Get your own hides burnt!

TING (more bacon)

CUPID: I know, Pip! Move! (draws back his arrow and fires)

TAMARA (getting the hang of the challenge and shaking the bottles for me; I fire with stunning accuracy.): Bacchus, you are amazing!

ME (winking at her much the same way I had toward Cupid when I'd stolen her): My dear, you ain't seen nothin' yet. (Popping more champagne tops than I have in centuries, the tips of my thumbs swell and blister after the prolonged strain. Cupid's situation is no easier.) **(Stagehands, feel free to focus solely on Cupid's suffering.)** (Our group inches forward for grueling hours – shown onstage as mere moments – until...)

(Stagehands, abruptly change the swirling blue-green light to fiery red and pull the billowing fabrics down through the stage line.)
(The lava wall suddenly drops, leaving behind its thin line of ash. I return to prose, as the two factions are reunited.):

"Pip! You're on fire!" Tamara shouted.
That bacon smell was no joke. Pip's wings may have been singed before, but they were legitimately on fire now. He looked like a two-pronged tiki torch. Cupid's eyes grew wide. Seeing it, Pip looked up over each shoulder

and promptly panicked. He flapped his wings wildly, inadvertently fanning the flames. I decided, before he did anything foolish like wrap himself around someone's neck while still ablaze, to pour half my bottle of champagne over him. The look of shock on his face, along with the resulting hiss of flame and splash of hooch, was very satisfying. Pip coughed and sputtered, but his flames went out.

I tilted the bottle to take a long draft and then raised it high. "What a harrowing adventure! Anyone else need a drink? Here you are, Tamara!" I placed a steadying hand on the small of her back before offering her the bottle, which she took gratefully for her own long swig.

Pip flew over to swill some rotgut of his own.

"Champagne does make for a fun time!" I said to Cupid with a smile.

Cupid frowned, furious. "You're over there drinking while I'm here slaving away like a bath house towel boy?!"

I had a lot of experience with towel boys, and they hardly slaved away around me. "Oh, share a drink with us. Rejoice! I brought down the lava wall and even returned Tamara to you."

His jaw dropped. Before he could speak, or the lovers embrace, restrictions for which I was eternally grateful, Tamara pointed ahead. We found ourselves upon the fire god's lair.

Chapter 18

THE CHEAT

We immediately stepped back. So focused were we on the lava wall's abrupt disappearance and my playful banter (which Cupid didn't think was so playful, judging by his thoughts) that we nearly stepped off the edge of a precipice. Pip especially needed to compose himself despite being airborne and in no real danger of falling – even with burnt wings. I suppose it was the shock of it all. Cupid was about to suggest that I lead the group with a giant step forward, but Tamara saw him open his mouth and put a quieting finger to her own. He needn't have looked so disappointed; I heard the unspoken insult regardless.

Pip settled himself, first emotionally and then physically, quite near the ledge. He lay on his stomach and inched forward. We followed suit to see but not be seen.

We were perched at the mouth of one of a dozen tunnels drilled high in the sheer rockface that towered over an enormous cavern. I recognized it. I'd stood on that floor 100 meters below, surrounded by that complex web of motors and cogs, and so I turned toward my companions, eager to see their reactions. They did not disappoint, slack-jawed and wide-eyed at what they saw below.

Vulcan's mastery was merely hinted at by the

mystifying machinery that spun and whirred so ferociously that we felt the vibrations even at our height. Lassoing the motors below were a dozen enormous, steel vats, squatting over white-hot fires and connected by pipes. A closer look revealed that the vats were actually brick-lined ladles, brimming with red-hot molten metal. This liquid metal bubbled and popped over the vats' edges. It splashed into the fire and into the many buckets of water littered everywhere at the ready. Steam hissed all around us. The terrible furnace that must feed these metalworks was nowhere to be seen.

I snickered aloud, and my companions' heads swiveled questioningly. We were clearly in the world's most prolific foundry and in impressive danger should we be caught trespassing. It could get ugly. Ha, ha! Our situation was thrilling!

A bellow from afar caught our attention. All eyes returned to the cavern floor.

Half shuffling and half running, snorting and rabid and looking every bit as grubby and unkempt as you'd expect an undergrounder to appear, approached one of the most powerful and justifiably angry gods of them all.

Vulcan, Master of Metal and Firekeeper of the World, was short, stocky, and heavily muscled from centuries of strenuous manual labor. His skin paled from perpetual lack of sunshine, yet it and his abundant red hair were coated in enough soot for him to be mistaken for a bear. Come to think of it, his shaggy, black-fur tunic already made him look like one. He certainly smelled like one, I recalled from our last visit, and the hump on his back made him sort of clumsy like one. Still, I'd rather wrestle a hundred bears than spend a minute in the ring with him.

Vulcan vaulted over a pipe connecting two ladles to stand right in the center of his metalworks. He bent to the ground to scoop a stray dollop of red-hot metal into his bare hands. It must have escaped a ladle. It still steamed. I imagined its heat disfiguring anyone else who might handle it and was strongly reminded of literary silversmith Johnny Tremain. Both Vulcan and Tremain toiled so that a man – or god – could stand up.

Vulcan stretched the molten metal dollop into a sharp pointer and swished it like a conductor's baton to cool it solid. He then bellowed for the "accursed trespasser" to be brought in.

He's seen us! Cupid thought with a gasp and shrunk back. He pawed at Tamara to withdraw from the edge. She didn't move.

"Don't be ridiculous, Cupid," I whispered in reply. "Vulcan can't see us way up here."

Cupid's brows dropped and furrowed. *Did I say that out loud?*

I turned my gaze to Tamara, whose slightly squinted eyes regarded me suspiciously. "I mean to say that I think we're safe to look over the edge."

Tamara looked back at Cupid before allowing her probing eyes to linger on me. She held her scrutiny a second too long, and I wondered if she hadn't guessed my secret, perhaps even experimented by thinking shocking thoughts of her own to test my reaction. I kept a mild, pleased look on my face, the sort of expression that any simpleton might have at the attentions of a beautiful young lady. It was the easiest acting I'd ever done.

"Ya dare ta invade my home agin?!" Vulcan boomed at a giant boulder being rolled in by humpbacked servants and guarded on all sides by impressive, solid-gold soldiers.

"Again?" Cupid thought and scooted back to the precipice to peer over. His long, curly, brown locks tumbled to either side of his face, and I imagined anyone looking up might think a sheepskin had been hung to dry.

"Ya wanted in? Well, now ya'll never LEAVE!" Vulcan thrust his new baton toward the petrous mass, and his servants took their hands off it. "Ya dirty," – Vulcan raised the baton and the boulder jounced over a pipe to join him – "NO good," – he stabbed the air with both accusatory forefingers, and the rock began to crumble – "CHEATIN'" – he pounded his temples with both fists – "HOOOOOOMEWRECKERRRRRR!!!"

The boulder collapsed in a heap, and something struggled to climb out from the rubble. Before it could stand, Vulcan raised a fist. Veins of molten metal from the ladles burst out of their confines and arched over the prisoner to form a frame like a fiery birdcage.

The reimprisoned jailbird roared in outrage. Cupid jolted and leaned further over the edge, squinting hard.

Vulcan lunged and limped his way toward the jail cell. Steam popped off his head like a fumarole – that's a vapor vent, for those unfamiliar with volcanic vocabulary. As Vulcan got angrier, the underground cavern shook more fiercely; fiery embers popped out of the rockface and rained down on him like snow in a snow globe.

(I really must remember these theatrics for my next production. The steam off his head would of course be shown by dry ice. Yes, the very dry ice that Cupid earlier didn't find worthy of attention. See how wrong he was? And the red embers? Why, short-stick sparklers of course.)

"Nuthin' worse'n a cheat!" Vulcan howled before pointing his baton at the feet of his dusty prisoner. Fissures cracked the ground around those sooty feet, and from the crags popped dozens of rough chunks of earth.

The captive took a step back, and his form was momentarily outlined by the blazing red of the molten bars. He was the large and muscular type, barrel-chested and, judging by the way he moved, agile enough to make a formidable enemy. He took another step back and singed a shoulder on the burning bars. He hopped forward with a shout, and the earthy chunks that Vulcan had called forth latched themselves to his ankles.

Do something! I heard Cupid think. I looked over to see my mental magnet rise to his knees. Then I looked back at Vulcan's unfortunate felon.

The chunks of rock transformed. Parts crumbled away, but other parts clung to the captive, who struggled to rip them away. The clingy globs spread like malleable dough to encircle both ankles, and then stretched to connect. The connecting wad further transformed into chain links, and the whole contraption immediately hardened into leg irons.

"Vu-u-u-u-u-u-u-u-lcan!" the hostage shouted.

I heard Cupid recognize the prisoner a fraction of a second before he cried out, "Dad!"

I leapt on the fool and covered his mouth.

Chapter 19

MARS' TERROR

S o now yu'll know, Mars, what the pain of adult'ry really is!" Vulcan boomed. He stretched high on the balls of his feet and howled like a mad dog. "Arrrroooooooo!"

I released Cupid, not to miss Vulcan's lunacy.

"Ya thin' ya kin use ma' tunnels ta get in! Ya thin' they won' trigger an alarm an' let me know! Well, *I* know! Soldiers!" He pointed to the vivified golden guards and then to the nearest cave. "Find any friends he brought along!" They scattered toward cave openings all along the ground floor. Thank the gods, it would take them some time to find us.

"An' you," Vulcan continued to Mars, "yu'll be trapped in this cage, like all adulterers oughter be, ferever! Da weight'a da chain'll hinder ya, like da weight of yer lies erodes the vows of ma lovely Venus. And to equal da pain ya put me through wih' yer whole affair, ha!, dat chain'll heat to burnin' each day at high noon. Yaha, look! Apollo mus' be reachin' da hump now 'cuz the iron's gettin' hot!"

The contraption turned from a dark grey to a lighter one. Cupid's eyes met mine. We knew the iron would soon be scalding red. It somewhat made sense that Vulcan would tie his punishment to the sun's course; spending so much of his life underground, he would find a romantic notion in heliolatry.

"Da chain'll char ya 'n cause sufferin'," Vulcan continued, "like the sufferin' felt by all the faithful lovers wonderin' 'bout the whereabouts 'a der two-timin' spouses. Yer days'll be insufferable, an' yer nights'll be sleepless while ya painfully heal 'n wait fer da next bout 'a pain, same as da innocents awaitin' the next bout 'a cheatin'. Ya got it comin', Mars, God of War! Mars, as adulterin' as yer father. Mars, who done me wrong. I'll stop yer meddlin' an' I'll be heralded a hero by jilted lovers ev'rywhere."

"Great gods!" exclaimed Cupid. "That's a punishment worse than Atlas'!"

"And yet just as deserved," I muttered.

Tamara was the only one who heard. She leveled a raised brow my way, as if disapproving, yet ... what else? Ah, yes. Conflicted. She couldn't disagree that tying the knot should cut off others' access. She looked away without a word. I marveled at her respect for truth. As attests Shakespeare, "truth is truth to the end of reckoning." That she was still single .... with that *je ne sais quoi*... amazing.

"We've got to stop Vulcan," Cupid hissed.

I dragged my attention back to fly boy. "Just wait."

"But," Cupid began.

"Wait," I commanded. "Others have talents, too."

We returned to our perchy edge and watched. The chain started to turn pink. Mars raised himself to full height, dramatically stretched his arms out to each side,

and, just when you thought he would do something amazing, clapped his hands together and stared at Vulcan. The
hand clap was unexpected and booming. It echoed off the
walls like cannon fire. But it did seemingly nothing else.

Ummm, Cupid thought. *What's that supposed to do?*

I agreed. Very auditorily impressive, but I hoped
Mars' talents extended further.

Cupid opened his mouth to ask what we should
expect now, to which I had no answer, but then something...
changed. Everything started to blur, as if we were looking
through heat waves. Then the cavern dimmed, as if the
white fires beneath the vats lost their will to shine. And,
just as I'd earlier sensed my favorite foods when Cupid
pushed Peace and Goodwill, I suddenly sensed danger
and warning and nondescript confusion. The god of war
below looked imposingly bigger.

"Oh!" proclaimed Tamara.

I knew. "The Terror of War." I turned toward
Tamara to explain more succinctly. "It's Mars' aura, his
version of Cupid's Peace and Goodwill. I imagine Mars
pushes it only rarely to up the ante in battle. The Terror
soon won't allow us to recognize that we're on the same
team." I removed my ivy-formed backpack once again
and pulled out my wine goblet.

"Wait a min', Bacchy," hissed Cupid, obviously
grown bolder and more foolish by The Terror. "I can jes
push Peace 'n Goodwill an' that'll counterac' Mars' move."

I had no idea he slurred when angry. Perhaps War deeply confounds The God of Love. "Cupid, my dear friend," I said soothingly, as I was not quite sure what kind of reaction I'd get. "If you counteract your father's talent, how do you expect that he'll escape?"

Cupid glared, and I went about my business of concocting a special wine mix before his father's powers overcame my senses as well. I pulled some ivy leaves off my tray and ground them into the goblet using my thumb as a pestle. I snapped my fingers to call forth some arrowroot from the nearby soil. The root flew to me, and I flicked my thumbnail across its skin to create shavings, which I drizzled into the goblet. I willed forth a sweet wine to counteract the bitterness of the ivy, stirred with my finger, and my brew was done in a snap. Years of experience will do that for you.

I took a massive gulp and then pushed the goblet toward Tamara, who'd been holding her breath. She accepted a gulp and stared into my eyes until I saw the transformation. She'd be fine. The cats lapped the rest, leaving none for Cupid nor Pip. Ah well, I reasoned. Time for melodrama.

It didn't take long.

Cupid shifted to face me. "I don't like you!" he declared loudly, stabbing his pudgy index finger into my chest. The Terror was clearly confusing him, I reasoned, as really I'd been quite kind to him thus far. I had barely applied myself to cultivating any displeasure, and, believe me, I could really apply myself if I let loose. Tamara turned to hide a grin which I nonetheless saw.

"Eeeeeeeeeeeeeeyah!" screamed Pip. "He'll burst the cage!"

Tamara and I looked down to see Mars standing center-cage and nowhere near big enough nor armed enough to burst through it. What an amusing little trick is Mars' emanation.

"Have you lost your mind?!" Cupid screamed at Pip. "Stop shouting!"

Tamara facepalmed herself.

I stowed my goblet. Our cover was seriously blown.

"Who dat?!" roared Vulcan, looking up and spinning on the spot to see within each tunnel opening. "I'll boil ya alive!"

"Oh, dear," I said with a sigh and patted Tamara's shoulder. "I had hoped to come up with a plan before we were discovered."

Cupid slapped my hand away. Tamara ignored her lover's hissy fit.

"We better show ourselves," she advised.

I nodded in agreement. "Mount," I said.

She swung a leg over the alpha panther as if she'd ridden wild animals all her life. I hopped on the beta cat and guided it to push Cupid toward the gamma. Cupid's knees collided with the third cat, and he tumbled onto its back, the cue for all three cats to leap over the edge.

Our free fall was magnificent, and I was strongly reminded of the striking 1970s velvet posters depicting black panthers against neon backgrounds. Our background was rock with falling red embers, and only one of our panthers carried a gorgeous black heroine. I imagined how she'd look with a traditional afro. Cupid really didn't merit that enchantress.

We landed gracefully and without a sound except for Cupid, who bellowed the entire way and rolled off his cat to smack the ground hard.

"Cupid, you have wings," I reminded him. I didn't bother pointing out that we didn't have to mount the cats at all except for effect. Which failed. Thanks to him. And thanks to Pip, who plummeted down, flapping his arms in hysterics to launch himself around Cupid's neck.

"Grphm," Cupid gurgled.

Vulcan thrust his hands toward the nearest vat. Then, with a hideous grunt, he swung his hands overhead and ended his arch pointing our way. Molten metal followed his command and immediately caged us. Pip's high pitch scream rivaled any dolphin's. Vulcan's humpbacked minions scattered. The Terror was clearly making everyone absurd.

Tamara looked around, her mind clear thanks to my protective potion. "Do you mind?" Tamara asked me courteously.

"You may always speak before me, my dear." Chivalry is not dead, you know.

Tamara dismounted her panther to address Vulcan at his level. "Hello, Lord Vulcan, majestic God of Fire and husband to Venus." She curtsied deeply. "And perhaps someday... father-in-law."

Vulcan jerked his neck back at a home invader addressing him so.

Cupid turned his head so quickly he risked whiplash.

Mars jutted his chin; I suppose *he* would prefer the title of father-in-law, as he was in fact Cupid's father, the legitimate one at least. Well, I guess *illegitimate*. Ay, these adulterous webs. I only hoped Mars could be reasonable enough to silence himself, as he was in need of help. The chains on his legs were starting to smolder.

"Is Venus here?" Tamara asked. "Cupid here has promised to take me to see her, haven't you, Snookums?" She turned to face the so-called god of love and ran her pointer finger down the side of his face, ending at his chin, before tickling under it in a most revolting, lovesick manner. She is indeed a fine actress. I hope.

"Well, you know," Tamara continued, turning back toward Vulcan, "Venus can be hard to find. She wasn't at her castle spa but, really, it does make more sense to find her here, doesn't it?"

Having been with Tamara long enough to begin

to know her mannerisms – but not nearly as long as I'd like – I noted her unnatural chattiness. She wasn't lying to Vulcan, but she was certainly trying to distract from the whole truth.

Mars spit on his ankles, hoping to cool metal that he was powerless to influence.

"Oh, we have so much to chat about," Tamara continued, "the three of us, I mean – you, Venus, and me."

"And, my old friend," I chimed in, realizing time was of the essence for Mars' sake, "it is time that you and I shared another drink. Perhaps you'd free me – all of us – for the purpose?"

Vulcan turned his fire-red eyes my way. Normally that would be reason enough to run, but I was probably the only one here that Vulcan liked, so I felt reasonably safe.

Vulcan shook his head as if trying to clear away cobwebs; Mars' Terror was robust. Cupid spread his wings and singed them on the cage. He did it twice more and couldn't seem to understand that he was causing his own agony. Pip had dropped to the ground at some point and was trying to dig his way out but had started at the center of the cage rather than an edge. Mars was grunting as even his war-hardened hide began to feel the burn's pain.

"Yer, yer – nooooo!" Vulcan boomed. "Yer with him!" He pointed at Mars. "Yer wantin' ta free him from his jes' deserts!"

"Vulcan, my friend," I answered coolly and honestly,

"we didn't even know he was here."

"Yus two deserve each other!" he shrieked, clearly miscounting the number of people in the room. He thrust both hands outward, palms facing each other, one toward each cage, and slowly drew them together. The cages shuddered before shimmying toward each other. Their inhabitants, we, were forced to move along until the two cages touched. The connecting spears of molten metal then raced outward to merge the cages into one.

"I dun captured me TWO homewreckers – an' da wors' a da lot! Who knows how men' relat'nships I'm savin'?!"

I had to hand it to Vulcan; he certainly had a good grasp of the situation. Nonetheless, I tried again. "Vulcan, you misunderstand our purpose here." Let no one say I deceived him.

Mars' protests grew louder.

Cupid looked round and round, overhead, and across the room, seemingly unaware of where he was.

Vulcan turned his attention to Cupid, whom he despised for merely existing, that Captain Cuddles being the carnal result of his wife's infidelity.

"Ya shouldn'ta come here," Vulcan muttered under his breath while rubbing his head. "Ya bastard, righ' in mah own home."

I gave a little ahem cough lest Vulcan forget the other god in the room besides the bastard son of his wandering wife and the bastard son of the Queen of the Gods. (Not that there's anything wrong with bastards. I'm one myself, and literature is full of the lovable scamps.)

"Would you kindly let the rest of us out?" I asked a bit forcefully. "I assume you didn't mean to ensnare us along with these homewrecking cellmates of ours."

"Hey!" Mars barked, and Cupid flinched at the noise.

"That's how he's referring to you two, isn't it?" I asked Mars in self-defense. "He didn't point fingers at me, you'll notice." (And after all, I could hardly be called the homewrecker here. I was the one who helped Vulcan get his bride Venus.)

Vulcan's nostrils flared with the expulsion of angry air. He shook his head hard to clear the effects of The Terror, and then the magma bars to my left dissipated. Tamara grabbed Pip by the wings, much the same way a child would snag a butterfly, and we and my three cats slunk out. The bars reappeared behind us before Mars, dragging Cupid by the arm, could hobble an escape. Mars' eyes flared in outrage.

The skin around the war god's ankles blistered under the now red-hot leg irons. His face contorted in pain, and the fire in his eyes very nearly matched Vulcan's. One could not shrug off such a look, but I nodded slightly to advise him, as I had his son, to hold on just a little longer for others to show their talents.

"Thank you, old friend," I offered Vulcan cheerfully.

Tamara got to her tiptoes to speak into my ear. "The Fates' warning," she whispered. *"A contender's under-mining mission / May steal my courter, my swain some night.'* Vulcan's undermining mission is to overtake Olympus, and he's trying to trap my Cupid."

Despite her topic of choice, her closeness was exhilarating, and I think it was she that made me yet again give Cupid a fighting chance. She'd need help. Cupid would never escape Vulcan's snare otherwise, nor would his father, not that either was necessarily deserving of being sprung from the charges against them, but, really, this feud between Vulcan, Mars, and Son had nothing to do with Tamara, and I'd hate to see her unhappy because of it. (Stagehands, if you wish to lower a traditional angel's halo from the rafters to hover atop my head, no one could blame you.)

Vulcan's minions screamed from the depths of various caves at some unseen threat. No doubt Mars was upping the Terror.

"Tell me, Vulcan," I intoned as if the fate of my companions were not terribly top of mind. "What's next?"

Chapter 20

THE SHELL GAME

C upid'll suffer jus' the same as his father," he crowed, shaking his head even more vigorously to fight the effects of Mars' Terror. Vulcan grabbed hold of a thin ring around his head and yanked it down. He repeated the act to secure it further, and it was then that I realized what I was seeing: his crown, the one we were after, thin as a string of spaghetti, black with grime, and nearly hidden in the matted, filthy red hair atop his head. I'd never seen it before, although he may have always worn it, even in my presence, and I'd never have noticed it had he not brought it attention, surely unthinkingly. He tilted the flimsy curio to a new angle before releasing it. "Cupid'll nev'r cheat on no one agin."

Cupid balked. I wondered how he'd even heard Vulcan through The Terror. Then I noticed that Mars still had him by the arm, perhaps shielding him from its effects. I heard Cupid's affronted thoughts before he spoke them (which is good because some people never think before speaking): *You filthy, hypocritical, foolish old GROUND WORM! Why aren't you furious at your adulterous wife?! Why can't you muster a sliver of anger toward her?!*

But he suppressed speaking these words, surely because he already knew the answer: Vulcan could never summon anger toward Venus, thanks to the power of her allure. Instead, Cupid's razor-thin reply concerned only his own actions. "I've never cheated on anyone that I've committed to."

"Cuz ya ain't never committed before, so it's easy to say, now ain't it?!" Vulcan retorted. "Ya' jes float from girl ta girl an' thin' it's alrigh'. But dem other gals ya've been with, some of *dem's* been committed, wadn't dey? Ya tempted 'em, Cupid. You an' yer teasin' mother. Had to catch bof 'a ya in my traps." He shook his head vigorously before dropping to a knee. The Terror seemed to be breaking through his defenses. "Ya'll cheat on poor Tam'ra, too, dat heroine we've hearda even here'n da depths a'da Earth."

"Not on Juno's Juju would I do such a thing!"

Vulcan flinched angrily, and Cupid realized too late that invoking Juno would not ingratiate him here. (What was that I was saying earlier about thinking before speaking?)

"Don' you say her name here!" Vulcan roared. "She treated me wors' den anyone!"

Cupid stood silent, but his thoughts raced. The bars. The vats. The height of the room. Tamara. He dashed from thought to thought for an escape plan.

Mars' Terror was waning under the scorching punishment of Vulcan's burning leg irons. Mars crumpled in a heap, letting go of Cupid's arm and grasping the fetters, only to equally burn his hands. Mars was really rather in danger of a painful eternity.

Tamara turned, I'm sure to lunge at Vulcan, but I grabbed the tops of her arms. She struggled to get past me. "Please stop this, Vulcan! Cupid is not your enemy! He's done nothing to you. And Venus wouldn't want you to hurt him or Mars or anyone!"

"Here, here!" I agreed, shoving Tamara aside and grieving the act. I grabbed the fire god by an elbow and steered him away from the cages, implying a need for privacy. In truth, I thought Cupid might need a few minutes to finish up his escape plan, assuming he was still working on one. My gamma cat followed me.

"Vulcan," I began, turning to face him so that I could see the cage behind his back. I hunted for an argument that would be gentle enough for us to stay friends yet long enough to give Cupid a chance. "Just how will you explain to Venus that you've imprisoned her son and, er, someone else who may deserve it but who will nonetheless be an awfully ugly centerpiece to a major room in your home? It would become awkward. Do you expect to forever keep your wife from this room? And if not, really, how will this look good for you?"

Vulcan lowered his eyes angrily, and I took the moment to look over his shoulder. Tamara had a bucket of water in hand and was just tossing its contents through the cage's bars. I slapped my hands over Vulcan's ears so that he wouldn't hear the splash.

"What'r ya' doin', ya fool?!" bellowed Vulcan. The water splashed and cooled Mars' leg irons just the tiniest bit.

I released my grip. "Mars screamed, and I didn't want the guilt of his agonized torture to torment you forever."

"But I wanna hear him suffer!" Vulcan protested. "I-" Vulcan began turning back to face the cages, but I grabbed his shoulders and swung him back my way.

"But imagine the misery of a house full of tortured screams!" I lamented, slapping a hand to my heart. "What sad music to envelop a happy home!" (Now I was *really* acting because everyone knew that *that* home with *that* bride would never be Vulcan's version of happy.) "What *you* should hear nightly are the dulcet tones of devout affection purred through the sweet lips of your darling beloved."

I heard Cupid wretch and thoroughly ignored him.

Vulcan huffed. The ground beneath him hissed while it expelled frustrated vapor. And then he began speaking, calmly at first, about his past emotional blows and family letdowns. His lament grew slightly louder and angrier with each injustice ticked off his fingers, like lashes across a bare back. I listened while surreptitiously watching Cupid wedge two arrows between his father's ankle and the fire-red leg iron.

That'll never do, I thought, continuing to nod and occasionally pat Vulcan on the hump. The old boy really did have something to complain about. Behind him,

Cupid gathered a ball of water in his hand and turned it over to Mars. Cupid re-wedged one arrowhead against his father's blistered skin and the other between it and the shackle. He nodded for Mars to dribble some water on the whole apparatus while he flexed his arrows side to side, straining the quickly cooled iron. The iron grew red hot a mere moment after each dousing, but both Cupid and Mars repeated the move, cooling the iron, flexing it, creating fissures of weakness. I was pleasantly surprised. Tamara continued to throw handfuls of water through the bars toward Mars' ankles. I finally heard a pop just as Vulcan's howling laments neared a crescendo.

"Tell me more!" I insisted. "Let it all out! It's not healthy to keep all that anger caged up!" Caged up. CAGED up. No one laughed. Well, I suppose no one noticed the irony. IRON-y. Ha!

Vulcan wailed louder about cheats. I quoted La Carré: "You do not need to remind me that man is not equal to his rhetoric!" Hypocrisy was our shared lament.

Cupid repeated the freeing act for Mars' other ankle, which was scalded to the point of devastation, before turning to his own blistering flesh. Tamara silently cheered him in the background. Pip hid himself under an over-turned bucket.

"Sufferin' constant attacks from insigh' my home and out! Even my nigh's is tormented by that idiotic messenger!"

My attention snapped back. "Wait. What messenger? Pip?"

"I don' know no Pip," Vulcan barked, clearly irked at the interruption.

"He's the little one you just released from the cage."

Vulcan nearly turned to see, but I dramatically waved my hands in front of my face, which forced Vulcan to study me, confused.

"Some other messenger?" I pressed.

"'Course!" snapped Vulcan. "That meddlin' Mercury, cons'antly trying ta invade m' sleep!"

I froze. How many minds had Mercury looted? Mine, the elder gods, probably Pip's, too, judging by his muttering while he slept in the crystal cave, and now Vulcan's? Mercury, the messenger god – and god of the unconscious – was up to something.

"But I fig'erd out a way ta-" Vulcan stopped himself. He had my rapt attention. "People won' leave me alone! Deceivers ever'where!" Vulcan cried, dropping his anguished face into this palms. I knew he'd reached his finale. It was a shame I hadn't watched his whole performance right from the start, but I had my own to plan. I looked back over Vulcan's shoulder.

Cupid, with Mars' forceful tugging, removed the final cuff off his leg. Both gods fell in a heap, still captive but no longer being branded. A start. Vulcan swayed his head in his hands, symbolically washing away the anger and pain. I pointed at Mars and dragged a finger across my neck, then at Cupid and nodded. They understood, and the air, previously oppressive and unsettling, changed to welcoming, even evocative. I smelled walnuts and fine cheeses and probably would have felt a great deal of love for everyone around me had my wine not shielded me from the full strength of Cupid's influence. I looked toward Tamara, who cupped one hand in front of her face and used the other hand's index finger to stir its imaginary contents. Ah, she saw my plan.

"What's that?" Vulcan whispered, raising his head to look me in the eye. "I smell sea foam and perfume and ... *Veeeeeenus.*" He sighed dreamily.

"My friend," I said while cuffing Vulcan genially on the shoulder. "Venus would not want to witness this scene, whenever it is that she might arrive." (Let no one suggest that I confirmed her immediate arrival; what Vulcan smells from Peace and Goodwill does not mean that I should lie to him.) "Vulcan, you must behave above the acts of others and continue to use your talents for good. Come now, release your captives, who've surely learned their lesson."

Vulcan nearly turned back to look. I swiveled him my way again.

"Mars is badly burned," I continued, "and will no doubt never return. Cupid and Tamara can have their long chat with Venus another day, and I'm sure Cupid will know better than to offend you with another unannounced visit.

Look not upon your troubles! Cast them and your cages aside! Come, let us drink!" I commanded and produced my goblet. I make a fine wine, if I do say so myself, and the fire god knows it.

Vulcan huffed again and waved his arm behind him. The cages soared upward and split into numerous arching streams of molten metal before splashing back into their ladles.

"Thank you, Vulcan," Tamara called with true sincerity.

Vulcan turned to see all as he expected: Tamara, Pip, and the cats unharmed; Mars and Cupid on the ground, rubbing their ruined ankles. Satisfied at his revenge, Vulcan answered, "You and those ... GODS with you ... and the others... may leave." He thrust a fist upward, and the cave roof above them broke apart, dropping boulders big as chariots all around them. When we looked beyond the storm of dust above, we spied a wide hole leading distantly to blue skies. The volcano's mouth.

Tamara mounted my alpha cat, and Mars the beta, while the gamma cat stayed at my side. Pip and Cupid spread their wings, and the whole group started upward while Vulcan watched. Only when Vulcan turned to face me again did Cupid veer off to hide in a tunnel. His work was undone.

And so once again, dear reader, it would be the power of wine that would save the kingdom, as it was clearly doing thus far in this tale. I called forth various roots and tubers, ground and cut their contents into my wine, and offered my potion to Vulcan.

"For renewed energy, should you need it," I offered with a wink. "To Venus!" His face opened with a wide smile before he took the drink and gulped it down.

"But, my, you are a mess," I said now that the effects of my wine were about to course through his system. I pointed at his hair. "Might I suggest you at least splash the dust off your head?"

Vulcan's eyes widened at the thought of his goddess seeing him unkempt, prone as she already was to wander. He whipped off his crown and peered at me. I turned my back to him, squatting to pet my cat and giving Vulcan a moment to himself.

Where he set his crown, I know not. A few moments later, I heard water splash behind me and assumed he'd dumped a bucket of water on his head. Not the most elegant way to wash oneself, especially with water of dubious cleanliness, but to each his own. At his loud grunt, I turned back toward him.

"Much better!" I declared in regard to his flattened, dripping mane. "One more drink before I depart, to soothe the nerves." I concocted more of the same as before, a potion of unfair potency, producing profound but temporary forgetfulness, much as wine is already apt to do. "To old friends," I toasted. "May our friendship outlast all adversity!" (And may his aversion to reading keep him forever ignorant of my complicity.)

I pretended to drink and then handed the goblet to Vulcan, who drew deeply. As I watched, I saw Cupid swoop to ground level far behind him. He bent down and shook something in his hand, releasing a small cloud of dust. Just as he spread his wings for takeoff, a flash of gold tackled him. Then another. In the span of a few heartbeats, no less than ten of Vulcan's solid gold servants piled on Cupid, I assume to reclaim their maker's crown. I could only thank our aristocratic nature that Vulcan made his minions mute. No one likes overly chatty servants.

They did, however, make some scuffling noises that almost drew Vulcan's eye.

"Oh, Vulcan!" I nearly shouted. "You're still a bit shabby. Let me fix you up!" With that I grabbed his fur tunic and shook him about a bit pretending to readjust it, babbling the whole time.

Cupid and the golden serfs were all out brawling. They rolled in a heap, and the domestics clattered together. Vulcan tried to turn again.

"Oh, my. My jewelry is noisy!" I lamented and pulled out my pocket watch, which had almost no chance of making noise. I looked over Vulcan's shoulder and saw Cupid kicking and punching. When he looked my way, I shot him an eyeful of "hurry-up-why-dontcha."

"You're almost ready," I chirped to Vulcan. I

grabbed his mane of hair and began fluffing it like a practiced stylist. There was no fixing that mess. In fact, I think
I made it worse. When I looked to Cupid this time, I saw
him hovering over two servants at a time, picking up one
in each hand, and flying them over to the molten vats.
They flailed. He released. Plunk, plunk.

"Argh, what're ya doin,' Bacchus?!" Vulcan howled.
He slapped my hands away and was half-way turned before
I grabbed his shoulders one last time and spun him around.
Cupid only had two more servants to dispatch.

"You're smudged, just there," I insisted. I licked a
finger and ran it down his sooty cheek, leaving a streak
that not only showed his true, pale skin color but was also
likely the cleanest part of him. Let that sink in a bit.

Over his shoulder, I saw Cupid, alone now, launch
himself silent as an owl upward toward the sky.

The shell game is the oldest performance in all
of theatre.

"But I linger too long, my friend," I said to Vulcan
as my departing words, "what with you washed and ready
for anything. As always, I wish you well."

I mounted my cat slowly, such that Vulcan would
see my every move. My cat sprang upward, grabbed the
rockface, and clawed his way up. It might be minutes
or days before Vulcan realized that his crown was gone.
But one thing was certain: as far as he knew, no one was
there to see where he'd hidden his crown, except me, and

he knew I saw no such thing. He saw me leave his home without it, and the drink would, at least for the next few hours, make him wonder if he hadn't simply misplaced it, if he thought of it at all.

By then, his crown would be in the unconquerable hands of Jupiter.

(Stagehands, tip a vat of orange paint across the tarped stage to represent lava -- and Vulcan. Little did we know we'd just harmed him in a way far more severe than simple theft.)

Chapter 21

CANTING

My cat and I broke through to the skies above and spotted three groups ahead. Cupid was nearest, although still far away, beating his snowy white wings. Those giant appendages, with their baby blue tips, looked rather graceful, I must admit, as did he, closing in on the second group, which, I could just discern, consisted of everyone else previously trapped by Vulcan. A third group, a faraway, dark mass, was coming in from the side. Squinting, I could see that it was Mars' red quadriga chariot pulled by his four magnificent black stallions.

I shivered. Those stallions always brought on the willies. They are massive and far more imposing than my panthers, which is surely the point. I'd still choose my pantira any day, as my cats are more approachable to potential love interests. I've never had a single "interest" disinterested, be they male or female, old or young; Tamara even had a cat favoring her over blissful solitude. Never before.

Faster, I heard Cupid urge himself on. *He'll try to run off with Tamara again if he reaches his horses before I get there.*

I tapped the side of my gamma cat, and he accepted the invitation to let 'er rip. I didn't want to miss anything.

My cat's full sprint was both exhilarating and a much smoother ride than a canter, to use equine terminology. Besides, if my cats were going to be compared to Mars' stallions, as was inevitable, they'd need to arrive in raging full force.

The three groups ahead nearly collided, as the stallions refused to slow in deference to anyone, and Cupid had his own concerns. Tamara looked over her shoulder past Cupid, toward me, heedful of my safety. Would that Cupid had seen such devotion.

I caught up with everyone and watched as Tamara's smile, no doubt springing from her happiness of seeing me safe, drooped at the growing intensity of the family squabble beside her.

"You'll lose your head over this, boy!" Mars warned. The panther he was riding stepped side to side, refusing to stay put.

"You said that about fighting Pluto, and look where I am now!" Cupid retorted.

"You had plenty of help, though, didn't you? And we were eager to help because you were defending yourself – and the kingdom – so you claimed. This time you willfully stole something from another god. I'm not blind, son. You went back and came out with that – that – whatever it is. Who's the warmonger now?"

"I *had* to get this!" Cupid protested.

"NONSENSE!" Mars boomed.

The panthers flinched.

The horses did not.

I hoped no one noticed.

Mars continued, "What did you *have* to get?!"

"I… I can't tell you," Cupid said with a grimace. *Although I'd love to rub it in your face that Jupiter chose me for a mission instead of you.*

"You can't just take things without inviting war," Mars admonished.

"Look who's talking!" taunted Cupid. "At least I only stole his crown and not his wife!"

"That's his crown?!" Mars demanded. "You stole Vulcan's crown?! You've gone mad!" He ran a hand through his thick, black hair. "It's all this *love* drivel! They say love makes you mad, and now we know it's true!"

"I'm not mad, Dad!" Cupid barked. "I just can't tell you what this is all about."

Mars turned to Tamara, who by now was watching the exchange with open dismay. If she married into this family, she'd also marry into their neuroses. Mars held out a hand to her in invitation. "Come along, my dear. Let me spare you from his ruin."

"Now who's mad?!" accused Cupid. "We just sprung you from a trap brought on by your own philandery!"

"That word does not exist," I offered helpfully.

"Well, it oughta!" Cupid cried with a wrinkled look of who-invited-you-to-this-party?

"You should know," I sang, happy to flame the fires.

Tamara looked my way with pursed lips but, yet again, could not argue truth. I liked that; she had yet to display the egregious trait of hypocrisy, the defining characteristic of man and god alike.

"What. Did. You. Say?!" challenged Cupid, taking a step towards me.

"Hmm, perhaps your father is right," I offered. "Perhaps you are warmongering, first with your father, then with me. Please don't go after Tamara next." I covertly nudged a knee into my feline's side so that it stepped toward her. It was brilliant; I was now near enough to "protect" her, yet it appeared as if the cat initiated the move.

"If he did, I could handle myself," warned Tamara. I looked over my shoulder to see her with a most uncharacteristic scowl. "Clear the path so I can see."

I made a show of patting my cat's other side so that, this time, the move clearly originated from me. "I am your servant."

"Her servant!" scoffed Cupid. "More like her abductor. You're just as much a thief here as the rest of us. My dad steals women. I stole a crown--"

"*And* women!" I interjected. Might as well stir some stuff up.

"Shut up!" answered Cupid.

"He's right, though," added Mars.

"And you stole Tamara from me in that cave!"

Cupid continued, choosing to not re-engage his father. That made sense; I was a much easier target than his gigantic, combative father.

"This is not helping at all," Pip piped in.

"Shush, Pip!" demanded Tamara.

I laughed in spite of myself. She'd rather the fight play out? And *I'm* the dramatist here?

"What's so funny, you kook?!" Cupid questioned.

I savored this volleying. It was hugely entertaining.

"Never mind that," Mars interrupted. "What's *he* doing here?" Mars pointed a beefy forefinger at Pip, who had suddenly turned neon green. "Anytime he's around, Jupiter's involved."

Pip puffed up his chest and spread his buggy wings wide. The green flashed brighter. "Cupid is not authorized to--"

"I didn't ask you, sissy!" bellowed Mars.

"Why I never!"

"And you never will if you don't shut up!" Cupid threatened.

"I-wha-?"

My alpha cat roared and swiped a paw Pip's way.

Mars turned back toward his son. "Cupid, you prat! The royals are using you to persecute poor Vulcan again, aren't they?"

"Poor Vulcan?!" Cupid wailed. "You victimize 'poor Vulcan' every chance you get with Venus!"

"All's fair in love and war, son. You've said so your-self, I believe, while conquering all those innocent lasses over the ages."

Cupid turned a sheepish eye toward Tamara.

"I'm not what I used to be," he answered calmly, for her benefit.

"I can see that, son! You're now a thief! And roping in your fine lady as an accomplice! Come, my warrior." He again extended a hand to her in invitation. "Real men won't steal what they want. They earn it."

Cupid balked. "What?! Then why won't you 'earn' Venus?!"

"Clearly I do if she keeps coming my wa-," retorted Mars.

"Earn Venus?!" interrupted Tamara. "Are you com-paring a living, flesh-and-blood goddess to a metal crown – a thing?"

Cupid's noose was tightening. It appears that he, like me, is an easier target than Mars.

"I – no. No! I just … someone who espouses war can't talk about nobility."

"And why not?" asked Tamara, putting her hands to her hips. (Gods, she was lovely.) "Mars is honest in who he is."

"Are you saying I'm not?" Cupid asked, offended.

"No, Sugar. I'm not saying that," she replied simply. "You just need to be careful how you phrase all this. The love triangle here is not just the result of Mars' and Vulcan's actions alone. Venus is a party, too, and a sentient being, not something to be earned or stolen. She's the goddess of love and beauty. It appears to me that she's honest in who she is. And Vulcan knew who she was then and who she is now. No one has to like the situation, but they've made their choices."

Cupid's confused thoughts ran round and round in his head so quickly they banged together and tangled like fishing lines.

Pip seized the silence. "Exactly! I was trying to say the exact same th-"

"SHUT UP!" Cupid shrieked.

Mars' horses whinnied angrily at Pip and popped fire through their nostrils.

Pip squawked and tried to hide behind Tamara's panther. It turned and swatted him away. Pip had turned black. I frowned at the transformation. Pip's coloring swung faster than a fiber optic lamp. Cupid watched with detached indifference.

"I'm still right," interjected Mars, to which particular point I know not.

Cupid glared at him before turning softer eyes to Tamara. "I-I'm lost," Cupid said. "What are we even arguing about?"

Mars snorted. "The stolen crown, which will get you boiled in oil if Vulcan finds out, but that's the battle you've chosen."

Cupid stared into the eyes of a god who had no intention of offering fatherly advice.

A standoff. Such a sad moment for a lover of drama such as myself, but the show must go on. "This disagreement," I said to the group at large, "is all chemical, you see. I suspect the effects of Mars' Terror of War are lingering on you, Cupid, and I further suspect that your father is still fired up from his confrontation with Vulcan. Perhaps you two ought to kiss and make up. Go your separate ways. You have no quarrel with each other." Sad but true.

Cupid and Mars crossed their arms like stubborn toddlers (as much as a colossal beast like Mars can look like a toddler), but they eventually nodded their apologies.

Mars put his hands atop the cat he was riding, popped up to standing, and jumped toward his chariot. Grabbing hold of a horn-like fandangle at its head, he swung himself in. He directed a wave at Tamara, shook his reins, and rode off, soon becoming a speck in the distant sky.

"Well, that was just ridiculous!" Pip assessed.

"No more ridiculous than you trying to *dig* your way out of an underground cave created by a mountain god," I replied.

Pip pouted.

"You tried your best," Tamara said to soothe him, then added to the group at large, "I think it's time we handed off this crown to Jupiter. The sooner it's out of our hands, the better."

"Absolutely," agreed Cupid, who flew over to plant a tentative kiss on her cheek.

I detected apprehension on that fair face, and I admit to feeling uneasy as well. Like Sherlock Holmes, I suspected I'd missed a clue, and I was quite certain that there was more to this mission than mere theft.

Chapter 22

QUICK DETOUR

S o it's on to Sydney and the anniversary ball?" asked Pip.
"Not yet," I answered to everyone's surprise.
"You three will notice that we are riding my panthers as if
they were horses, something we've done twice in two days.
Not even your father rides his stallions, Cupid. If I expect
my panthers to stay wild – and they are wild, Tamara – I
cannot let them be ridden like pack mules. We must
retrieve my chariot first."

"No," Cupid protested. "The ball starts at sunset.
That's just a few hours away. We should get there before
all the guests do. If you want us off your precious pets,
fine. We can fly."

"You misunderstand, Cupid," I replied. "The chariot is also a space to conceal the crown when we arrive. Or
are you planning on telling the crowd assembled outside
– a very gossipy crowd – that the head ring you're carrying
is part of your costume?"

Sisyphean snake, I heard Cupid call me. *Compli-
cating this for no reason. Or, maybe he's hoping for more time
with Tamara.*

He wasn't wrong that I'd always love that.

"I don't need to hide it," Cupid retorted aloud. "No
one will know what it is. I'll just sling it over my shoulder."

"Like a purse?" I hooked my thumbs under the vines at my shoulders.

"Who's carrying the bag around here?" Cupid demanded.

"Mine's a backpack."

"Cut it out, you two," Tamara chided. "Bacchus, couldn't you just put the crown in your bag until we're standing in front of Jupiter?"

"I'm not entirely sure we want to be standing in front of Jupiter with it," I answered. She furrowed her brow, and I replied, "Never mind. We just have a lot to figure out here. There's also the issue of my thyrsus. It's wedged in the rock, remember, where I left it when I turned around to help Cupid. It can't come to me now and I can't leave it underwater being battered by salty seas. Above everything, though, my thyrsus could come in handy."

"How?" asked Cupid, threading his arm through Vulcan's crown and shouldering it.

"A staff is always handy," I replied.

"Oh, honestly!" Pip groused.

"Bacchus' thyrsus guided us to Venus' cave," Tamara reminded them in my defense. "If Bacchus wants it, I think we should go back and get it. It wouldn't take long, would it?" Tamara gave me a pointed look, which I nonetheless would have scaled mountains to see.

"But a moment!" I assured her. "In and out. Lickety-split."

Cupid looked back at Tamara and saw her reasonable countenance. "Fine," he muttered. "Tell these cats of yours to turn us around."

"I do not direct them, Cupid," I corrected. "I offer them to come along, which they choose to do because I treat them with respect. Were I to dare rule by force, I have no doubt that they'd relieve my body of the weight of my head."

And what a loss that would be, Cupid thought.

More loving thoughts from the love god. He must reserve his sincere affections for Tamara. She, the object of my tender thoughts as well, leaned forward to whisper in her cat's ear. Within moments, the alpha turned westward to occidental Sicily, the subordinates following suit.

We'd be there in minutes, and so I chose to give them something to ponder. "You know how skilled a thief is Mercury. So much so, that one must wonder why Jupiter didn't employ *him* for the task. Unless his fame is the very problem. If something were to show up missing, he'd be the first one suspected."

Tamara and Cupid turned wary eyes my way.

A quick reminder, my dear reader, should you have forgotten your bedtime stories. Mercury's is most remarkable. The god of thievery and commerce is, of course, yet another illegitimate son of Jupiter, begotten this time through the Titanic daughter Maia. Mercury was born the very morning after conception, and so, his understandably exhausted mother bound him in swaddling clothes so that she might rest, but Mercury proved to be most needy of supervision.

The moment his mother's eyes closed, the little god squirmed himself free from his swaddling clothes and was off. By noon, he'd killed a tortoise and used its shell to invent the lyre, which he immediately mastered. By nightfall, he had traveled no small distance to steal his half-brother's cattle. He was only saved Apollo's righteous chastisement by trading his lyre, which the god of light seemed keen on, for the cattle. The swap was Mercury's first hustle and the start of his wheeling and dealing.

In the years to come, the growing god stole Vulcan's tools, Venus' bridal belt even as she held him, and finally Jupiter's sceptre. Mercury's sticky fingers would have made off with the king's thunderbolt, too, if it hadn't proved too hot. For all the wronged gods, retrieving their stolen items was always a matter of negotiation.

Eventually fed up with the boy's criminality, Jupiter decided to employ him as a messenger. The king supplied his son with his now symbolic winged hat and shoes, which not only make the boy faster but help him in his other capacity as conductor of the newly dead to the infernal regions.

Rumor had it that Mercury raged for weeks when Cupid took Cerberus from The Underworld, as that left the region's borders unprotected. Hordes of dead escaped, and it was up to Mercury to drag them back. Come to think of it, Mercury was raging about more than the dead; he raged about mismanagement of the living. The gods always find something to rage about.

My panthers suddenly slowed, and I found us hovering over the same patch of Tyrrhenian Sea in which we'd earlier nearly drowned. I stared Cupid down.

Oh my gods, he expects me to go back in there, Cupid thought.

"I do not," I replied absentmindedly. Cupid's double take made me add, "expect you to re-enter the water. I see your hesitation, conflicted as Laertes toward his once-friend Hamlet. But soft, Cupid! I ask for no such vengeance. Merely an air bubble, if you would be so kind."

It took a moment for Cupid to recover from my literary reference. Eventually he rolled his eyes and swirled his hands to create an air bubble around my head. A perfect, transparent sphere. That's one small step for godkind.

Emulating the exit of the God of War, I planted my hands atop my panther's back and popped to standing. Then, spreading my arms wide, the better for Tamara to see my magnificent daring, I sprang forward to complete an exquisite forward dive.

Once again, the cold water assaulted my senses. I repeatedly pulled my arms through the water to descend. No mermen materialized from the darkness, although I suspected they would arrive en masse should Cupid repeat his trespass.

I felt the vines of my backpack partially disengage to wave behind me and assist my swim. I smelled the sea's fishiness even through my watery helmet. I saw only blackness. Perhaps it was the vines or perhaps the water fought me less; this swim seemed considerably less fatiguing than the last. Just as my deltoids began to tingle from exertion, however, a light flared ahead. My thyrsus.

I swam hard. When I was within arm's reach of it, the staff shook and struggled against the rock. I grabbed hold and yanked it free. In an instant, I found myself hurtling down the rockface, the divine rod dragging me in a most disconcerting direction, until we nearly collided with the chariot, which was propped against the outcropping where it had crashed. I stepped inside it and commanded its ascent.

As I rose, I once again heard Cupid's thoughts. *Shouldn't be here,* he fussed. *Too close to the water,* he brooded. *Get off me!*

I must have ignored his fretting while swimming. Or perhaps I was out of range, like a radio outside the listening area. His silence was a nice break, to be honest.

I neared the surface. My thyrsus pushed through, then my head, my chest, and finally the whole chariot. Salt water sluiced all around me, tumbling back into the sea. My cats sprang toward the divine transport, anxious to be free of the burdens on their backs and to re-attach themselves to the reins.

Tamara took the hint and hopped into the chariot, splashing the water at its base. Cupid took no notice, trying as he was to push away Pip, the tiresome gnat, who was re-riveting himself to Cupid's neck. Cupid managed to shove him aside and vaulted toward Tamara. The moment he splashed into the chariot, however, his face changed. Cupid looked down to see his feet submerged in three inches of water, which immediately thrashed. Cupid thrust out his wings to fly just as a giant blast of water hurtled up from below. It flipped the chariot and sent Tamara, Pip, and me tumbling. The cats rolled in its wake. The smell of fish was overwhelming.

"TAMARA, FLY!" Cupid shouted through the spray.

I looked through the vapor to see Cupid's terrified face as the water wrapped itself around his feet and pulled downward, providing Cupid with what might be his last view of the airy world.

Chapter 23

THE TRUTH RINGS THROUGH

The crown! Cupid thought.

I realized with awe that, despite the tumult and peril all around, his first thought had been to protect Tamara and his second to protect the kingdom.

The sea swirled around his feet like a snake, dragging him downward.

Cupid thrashed, struggling to free his legs. He slapped his wings against the grappling water but could not fight its power for long. His feet were pulled into the sea.

"Bacchus, catch!" Cupid bellowed and ripped the crown off his shoulder. His wings battered the frothing waves.

The sea tugged Cupid in, up to his waist, his chest. The time to throw anything anywhere passed.

Air! he thought.

He swished his arms overhead, and, with that single move, dropped the crown atop his head and shaped a water bubble from the neck up. I watched in stunned paralysis as the last bit of him – and the crown – disappeared into the sea.

"CUUUUUUUPID!" Tamara screamed – with an anguish I'd never imagined. **(Sound Techs, set the audio of her cry to 'Reverberate' mode.**

Let it echo as fiercely in the mind of the audience as it did across my soul.)

My heart cracked. I looked at Tamara's face, that treasured face that I'd dared to imagine calling my own, and knew in a moment that the curtain had dropped.

Yet I would do anything for her. I followed her eyes to the churning tide and knew not what to do nor how to save her Cupid from a watery death, but I did know I could do nothing for her happiness above water. I ripped off my backpack, and, with new reason for a heavy heart, I commanded its vines to stretch and hollow.

"Add to your lengths," I commanded. It would kill them.

They unweaved themselves, and I snagged Diana's Orb, my ambrosia tray, and my wine goblet before they fell into the sea. My vines stretched themselves long, then quivered in deathly obedience before blowing their light green innards to the far end. The resultant mass of xylem twisted like wool at a spinning wheel, lengthening itself like yarn. It spiraled tightly along the edge of the vine's stem to extend the length. I bowed my head in sorrow. In a murderous mere moments, my vines had gutted themselves, providing me a reasonably long air hose to perchance help Cupid. (Stagehands, paint a garden hose a darker, much lovelier green and here lower it from the rafters - but slowly. Allow my devastating performance to move the audience.)

Tamara swept over and threw her arms around my neck. "Thank you! Thank you!" she cried.

Too soon, my beloved, I thought in reply.

I slung my tray toward my chariot, which was righting itself. I tossed over the goblet underhand, confident it would safely reinsert itself into the side's silver casting. Then I passed my Orb to Tamara, in part to give her a responsibility that would free me to work. I was shocked to see her immediately toss the Orb to Pip. He was unprepared for the magical relic to be tossed his way; he yelped and flapped out of its path. I gasped, as did he, when the Orb flew past him and fell, on the verge of being lost forever.

Pip dived for the rondure and managed to put his hands around it just before it touched the blue, where Triton would surely claim it as booty. Pip struggled mightily with it. It was larger than he, but he shook his buggy, translucent wings and turned toward my chariot, likely to place it within.

I didn't watch.

"Far end, stay above water!" I commanded and snagged the vine's nearer end. I put it to my mouth and dived toward the swells. Just before hitting the surface, I felt arms wrap around my middle. I looked to find Tamara, diving with me, her face scrunched in desperation. Of course she would not stay behind. I kept my eyes on her troubled face until the brine blurred my vision. **(Stage-hands, hoist high the cardboard waves from below stage.)**

Had I the ability to speak underwater, I'd have asked what exactly she planned to do and how she intended to help. But I knew no better myself. I assessed the question as hypocrisy. And so we swam as one.

It took but mere moments, Tamara and I sharing the makeshift air hose, before we reached the spectacle. Cupid, to my great surprise, was not dragged to the deepest of abysses to suffer a dreadful and dark demise. Instead, the water barb that had dragged him into the brine now held him just below its surface.

I wondered why until I saw Triton's approach.

The son of the sea god charged from the gloom, riding side-saddle atop a great white shark. His double-fluked tail was even more muscular than the shark's and his countenance meaner. The barnacles clinging at his shoulders rippled at the fast approach. He drew his famed, horned conch shell to his lips and blew.

The tumult this caused, the horrid gurgling and scrapes, were sounds that had never before assailed my ears. The hail drew all manner of frightening fish to the charge: large-finned swordfish, sharp-toothed lancetfish, and long-tentacled jellyfish joined en masse. Behind them surged undulating waves of eels and multi-colored sea slugs, emerging like phantasms from the chill. It would horrify any who fear marine life.

I suddenly understood why Triton kept Cupid to the shallows: for the sunlight that could penetrate but a few feet into the sea; for the theatre of it, so that Cupid would see the terror to befall him while just out of reach of life-saving oxygen. Cupid's dome – trapping too little air – would only hold as long as his strength, which perversely would only last as long as his oxygen.

Tamara snagged the vine from my mouth and sucked in enough air to form bellows of her cheeks. She lunged forward and beat both her arms and golden wings. The flecks of red on those golden pennons glittered as she struggled to make headway. I lunged forward to do the same.

We made no progress. I looked toward Triton to see him holding his hand, palm-out, our way. We, like Cupid, would see but not advance. Triton's throng of sea creatures swam a wide, encircling ring around us. **(Stagehands, create a large mobile with cardboard cutouts of sea life. Spin the mobile in the rafters and lower the stringed animals nearly to the point of scraping the stage; the actors' faces must be seen.)**

Triton slid off his shark, and it darted into the circle of fellow watery beasts to bite the end off a tuna. Apparently, the beast's ferocity could only be subdued for its rider. Triton made no motion to curb its nature. Instead, the sea godling waved his massive double-fluked tail to position himself well within Cupid's line of sight and glared down his nose at his captive.

"You dare to claim heirdom."

His voice was most unnatural, not heard through the ears but more felt in the bones as clicks and thrums vibrating past the flesh to our skeletal frames. (Pit Orchestra, play a deep base to rumble through the gallery.)

"What are you *talking* about?!" Cupid asked angrily, his voice muffled and echoing in his tiny, domed quarters. "Who's claimed heirdoms?"

Triton raised both arms. The water that held Cupid spumed up, out of the sea, and, moments later, dragged him back in.

Cupid shouted something; I couldn't tell what, but I was shocked to hear no thoughts from him. No cursing. No outrage. Nothing.

Cupid gulped air, his eyes revealing surprised relief. Was he allowed a freshening dose of air? I wondered. Tamara swam back to me for the same.

"Only the lines of Neptune, Pluto, and Vulcan are worthy," Triton proclaimed, the water nearest his mouth rippling in vibration. I questioned if such a pelagic person could be heard above water. "Not your false line, your *half* line. You! Pretender to greatness!"

Tamara and I exchanged glances, knowing the egotist would disapprove.

"Pretender to greatness?!" Cupid bellowed in his airy cupola. "The world revolves around *love*! Therefore the world revolves around *me*, you fishy fanatic! You've got water on the brain! Let me go!"

Cupid thrashed wildly. I wanted to shout to him to preserve his energy and air, but I had no water dome to allow speech.

Triton brought his arms forward and then lowered them a fraction of an inch. The tentacle of water encasing Cupid's feet obeyed and lowered the love god about six feet. It stopped when his face reached the very limit of the sunlight's penetration. Cupid's eyes darted wildly.

So much, I thought, for Cupid, that reigning royalty of rapture. I hoped he would give up on explaining his superiority and would instead think up an escape plan, but I heard no thoughts.

"So you'll drown me, you coward?!" Cupid's widely stretched mouth indicated that he'd shouted, but I barely heard him, muffled as he was. I saw a change in his eyes, though. Fear. He was again running out of air.

I looked up to the water's surface and saw a shadow flitting across it, small as a bird. A larger mass hung high above. My chariot and cats. I considered demanding the lot fall onto Triton, but I knew he would simply dodge both before crushing them to the depths.

"Your arrogant charms have swayed King Jupiter," Triton boomed, sending a pulse through the water, "but ascension in Olympus belongs to pure lines. We sons of Neptune demand dominion *beyond* the seas!"

I would have choked on the arrogance displayed had I not feared actually choking to death underwater. The seas are the vastest dominion on Earth. To desire more seemed, well, grabby. But a moment's contemplation helped me understand. Neptune alone rules the seas, without the help of his many sons and daughters. His heirs certainly inherit privileges, but what and when might Triton rule any territory of his own if he does not take such territory from another?

As I exercised my brain on these keen observations, Tamara exercised action. She swam ten meters toward Triton, pulled her bow around her shoulder, wrenched an arrow from her quiver, and drew it, ready to fire. Disaster. Her movement caught Triton's attention. He flicked his wrist and she was immediately caught in a newly materialized rip tide. She struggled to hold her celestial tools while the current pulled her with the power to tow for miles.

I thrust out both arms, one to summon my thyrsus and the other to snag Tamara. I glommed the tip of Tamara's wing as she was about to tumble past. I ripped out feathers but managed to wrest her to my side just as my thyrsus, diving from above, pierced Triton's side.

The sea spirit wailed in pain. His loss of focus, a

mere moment, was enough time for Cupid to kick free. Even with the water shaking all around us, Cupid paddled and scratched with every limb and wing until he broke the surface.

Tamara slapped my shoulder and pointed to Triton, who was extracting my thyrsus from the new, gaping wound in his torso. He dropped my celestial tool, and I watched it begin to sink anew.

Triton's inky blood diffused into the murk around him. He lurched toward the churning mass of sea creatures and pointed into it. A foot-long sea slug, blue and yellow, wiggled its way toward him and plastered itself against his wound. A living bandage.

At Triton's momentary distraction, I called forth my drifting thyrsus. It could pull us further away from Triton and away from harm entirely if necessary. I decided that, no matter Cupid's fate, Tamara would not come to harm. Cupid would want it that way. (Lighting Crew, a spotlight of warm yellow would aptly fit such altruism.)

As my thyrsus reached my hand and Tamara offered me another breath of air, a sudden collapse at the surface shocked us both. My panthers had plunged into the sea atop the far end of the ring of sea creatures. My eyes grew wide as they scattered the smaller fish and sank their claws into the larger.

A movement drew my eyes back to the principal.

Triton paid no heed to the chaos and coasted back toward center circle. He raised a fist and plunged it downward, re-snagging Cupid with a watery talon and dragging him back underwater. Cupid looked different in his bubble somehow; it took but a moment to realize that the crown was gone. I watched Cupid whip his bejeweled bow off his shoulder, draw its string, and fire a fast dart.

His arrow pierced Triton's torso just opposite my strike and exited his back. Triton clasped a hand to the laceration in obvious surprise. His eyes alighted on Cupid, and before he could react, something bright plunged into the waters between them.

The thing shone like a lighthouse beam. It pulsed light. As I squinted into the sun-streaked gloom, I discerned that it was round. Vulcan's crown. I looked from it to Triton and then Cupid. Only two gods here knew its value, and I was aghast to see that one looked intent on destroying it.

I watched in dismay as Cupid's eyes narrowed and he drew another arrow. Not even above water could I have shouted *no!* before he released that rocket toward the ring. In a single moment and with a horrifying blow to the gut, I realized that I'd miscalculated. I'd chosen the wrong actor. Cupid, my supposed savior and revenge, would destroy the ring, the reason for this mad mission, rather than allow it to fall into the hands of anyone but Jupiter's, no matter the cost to his own safety. This drama had turned serious.

In the heartbeat that it took me to analyze my misstep, a second arrow took flight. Tamara's. Toward Triton.

I watched both arrows at once. Cupid's struck the crown's inner edge and ricocheted through it (Yay! He missed destroying it!) to bury itself in Triton's side (Yay! A lucky bounce!). When Tamara's arrow hit Triton, it split Cupid's down the middle. (Yay for her always infallible aim!)

Yes! Cupid thought as he fisted the water in exhilaration.

Triton lurched.

I took the moment to turn my attention and found a horror befalling my panthers. Their blood stained the water around them. My gamma cat's side was pierced as if run through by a swordfish. He struggled to surface even as dozens of conger eels wrapped their full ten-foot lengths around him and his brethren. They'd drown my cats!

Ignoring the attack against Triton, I called forth seaweed and only hoped that the sea god was too busy or injured to override my command, as he surely could. My cats were losing strength and nearly overrun when the dark green ribbons of seabed algae that I called unfurled themselves from the depths.

They wrapped themselves around the eels and squeezed with all their might. The trapped eels immediately released my panthers, wiggled themselves free, and fled to the gloom from whence they came. I commanded my thyrsus to assist my gamma panther. I watched just long enough to see it hook the cat's forelegs and heave upward.

The wall of sea creatures fell apart.

I turned to find Tamara still at my side and Vulcan's crown at center circle, jolting this way and that. It followed Triton's erratic movements, which weren't the sharp ones of escape attempts. Rather, Triton seemed unsteady, confused. He brought his hands to his ears and shook his head from side to side. He focused to avoid the mysterious ring and then frowned at the scene before him. He retreated hesitatingly toward the gloom.

Cupid drew another arrow and tensed every time the crown flashed, but he fired no more.

I looked closer at that crown. It hadn't flashed on Vulcan's head nor on Cupid's shoulder. It was on the final flash before a bewildered-looking Triton lost himself in the murk that I saw what that flash really was. Pip was going from sea blue to white and back again. He commanded his coloring as first camouflage, then beacon, and he conducted his apatetic power to the metal.

"Let's go!" Cupid shouted in his bubble dome.

We shot up like corks in a barrel.

Cupid's head broke the surface first. His air bubble popped. *Victory!* he shouted in his head.

I nearly choked on sea spume. I couldn't believe what I was just figuring out. Of course, there had been no previous chance to understand. But now I did. How amazing.

The secret to Vulcan's highly sought crown was obvious, now that it revealed itself in action. The crown kept me from hearing Cupid's thoughts – or, more accurately, kept me out of his head, kept me from reading his mind, just as it would keep anyone else from reading Vulcan's.

Chapter 24

PIP'S TRUE COLORS

We flew to the chariot for our getaway. My cats wiggled into position at the reins and began to haul it, jerkingly, seriously injured as they were. They hobbled to put a bit of distance between us and the battle scene. Pip gabbled during the entire withdrawal from Triton's theatre about what a fine team he and Cupid make. When my cats faltered in their step, I called for them to halt. I then leaned over the side of my chariot and tugged my ambrosia tray from its casted walls. Just as I took off toward my cats, I caught Cupid's covert move of hooking Vulcan's crown inside the chariot.

Tamara followed me. She took over my tray as I tended to my suffering friends, feeding them with one hand and using the other to rub the delicate food of the gods over their wounds. They would heal, and we had to go further – and farther – quickly.

Cupid soared to me and stuck his face in mine. "Are you happy? You traitor. You nearly got us killed!"

I paused my ambrosia massage to give Cupid a most incredulous look before returning to my cats, who needed more attention than he. I shoved ambrosia squares into their already stuffed mouths. We couldn't linger. When I was satisfied that they'd be strong enough for an escape, I returned to the chariot. Everyone understood the unspoken directive to follow. Pip poised behind me. Tamara descended beside me, perhaps selecting the spot in expectation of her boyfriend's lunacy. Sure enough, he had no choice but to alight behind her. I raised a hand to request our departure. The chariot heaved forward as the cats, still recovering, pulled their charge.

"Well?!" Cupid asked as the jostling settled.

I would not allow Cupid to draw me into another long argument. However. The chariot bumped along. "Why exactly am I to blame for your near death?" I asked somberly, refusing to raise my voice. "Triton was angry with you well before I stepped onstage. Or have you forgotten his pursuing you to the Cyclops' cay?"

"Of course I haven't forgotten," Cupid retorted sharply, "and that was another instance where you didn't help me. Just now, though, did you hope to get me killed so that you could deliver Jupiter's prize to him yourself?"

(Tympanist, if you please, a roll on your largest, deepest kettledrum to express the gravity of such a shocking accusation.)

I stood in the skirring chariot, appalled that my intentions had been so badly misinterpreted. Cupid suspected me of true villainy rather than mild histrionics. I looked at Tamara's radiant face beside me and found it decidedly cloudy. She would not take more of our team's descent into dissent.

"The rather large point you're missing here, Cupid," I said as we glided along, "is that we learned the secret of the crown."

Cupid's bushy brows knitted in confusion.

"Let's review," I bade professorially. "What happened back there after you went up for air and Triton yanked you back down?"

"I hit him with an arrow."

"To little effect," I pointed out.

"There was some effect," he retorted.

"And so you struck again," I continued. "But this time you hit the crown first. Why?"

Cupid's brows unwrinkled, his anger ebbing.

"I believe I can answer that," Pip interjected, "if you don't mind the interruption, Mr. Cupid."

Cupid paused but, perhaps recognizing Pip's achievements of the past 36 hours, nodded.

"You see, you wouldn't know this, Bacchus, but when we were in Vulcan's cave and our two groups were separated by the lava wall, Cupid broke up the lava shoots on our side by striking them with well-aimed arrows."

I feigned surprise.

Pip went on. "He had me find the shoots just as they were forming-"

Tamara's head swiveled my way and I felt suspicion ooze all over me like an egg dropped on my head.

"-and hover in front of them so he could aim toward me. Well," Pip added, "I performed the same act underwater just now with Triton. I knew Triton was trying to escape Cupid's counterattack, and so I held the crown and even managed to light it to help Cupid know where to aim."

"And just how did you manage such an impressive light show, Pip?" I asked in the hopes of drawing away Tamara's piercing stare. It worked. She pivoted her eyes to look at Pip over her shoulder. She was as curious as I was, having watched his color change over the course of a day and a half.

"Well, again, sir, you wouldn't know, as you weren't there, but back when Cupid broke into Jupiter Heights – to save the kingdom, mind you – I sounded the alarm. Our King Jupiter was so pleased with my vigilance that, after Cupid's reinstatement, he bestowed a gift, one to better help me dispatch my duties as a royal messenger. I'm supposed to be able to control color."

"Say what?" asked Cupid. I saw Tamara raise a single brow.

"Not all color," Pip added quickly, waving his hands in amendment. "Just my color. To camouflage myself if I have to deliver a message to a god who might pretend to not be home when he sees me coming. I see now, though, that I radiate color, as well. I admit that I don't really have a handle on it yet."

"Ah, that's why you've been flashing like a rainbow these past days," I said.

Pip flushed like a teenaged mortal embarrassed by his voice cracking. He cleared his throat. "Yes, Bacchus. I suppose so. I couldn't control it."

"Well, you certainly did when it counted," Tamara noted.

"Yes, I did, didn't I?" Pip replied happily. "But Bacchus asked why Cupid hit the crown. I must have been so concentrated on giving Cupid a lit target that I failed to hold a steady hand. I must have moved it."

"No way. Not each time," Cupid assured him. "That crown's magnetized. It drew the arrowhead."

To test his theory, Cupid recovered the crown from inside the chariot and tapped it to his quiver. The arrows within shifted its way.

Tamara tilted her head in contemplation. I saw my chance.

"I see," I explained. "Your arrows, Cupid, striking Vulcan's crown, were presumably enriched by its power."

My celestial companions turned to me for more.

"What power?" Tamara asked.

"I believe the crown protects the mind – or breaks others' hold on it."

Cupid tensed.

"Explain, please," Tamara pressed.

"Well, as I said before, Cupid's first arrow did little,

but the second, the one that hit Vulcan's crown, had a noticeable affect. Triton's confusion was evident. His retreat was real, almost as if he didn't understand the battle befalling before him. Let us test this theory."

I pulled my wine goblet from the chariot's side and summoned within it a sweet, heavy wine. I turned around to offer it to Pip. "Drink. It will induce sleep."

Pip recoiled. "I don't want to sleep."

"The mission depends on it," I insisted.

Pip looked toward Tamara, his potential defender, but she nodded in approval. Pip turned to Cupid but quickly understood the futility in finding contradiction against Tamara there. He sighed, surrendered, and flew into Tamara's arms. I immediately sympathized. It would be a safe place to sleep – and a most wonderful place, at that.

Once he'd settled in like a naked, skinny baby doll, he reached forward to accept the goblet and a few hearty swallows. Within seconds, his eyes lost focus. His lids dropped, and he spoke.

"Hmmm, yes, Sire," Pip mumbled. "We … mmm… we have it. We're … nngh… on our way to you at the Opera House."

Tamara gasped. Cupid blustered in outrage.

"I heard him muttering in his sleep in the treasure room," I explained. "It sounded like a one-sided conversation, and I was strongly reminded of recently seeing others with royal connections talk in their sleep. I helped

Pip end that conversation. Now let's see if the crown does the same thing in this instance. Cupid, the crown please."

Cupid reached down to where he'd hung it and handed it over, his jaw set.

"Thank you." I nodded toward Tamara, and she slipped a hand under Pip's arm and lifted half of him like a rag doll. The move allowed me to slip the crown around him like a magician's ring. The mumbling instantly stopped. I raised the crown above his head once more and the mumbling resumed.

"Zzzz… yes, I'm here… zzzz."

I leaned down to whisper into Pip's ear. "Tell him to go screw himself."

"Szzz, go screw yourself," he hummed.

Tamara and Cupid exchanged glances of incredulity: open mouths, angry brows. I do so love a story's big reveal, especially when I have a hand in it *and* it relieves suspicion off me.

While the twosome gaped at each other, I leaned over the chariot edge and poured the remaining wine concoction into the sea below us, which we were quickly leaving behind, my cats regaining strength with each passing second. I called forth a new wine and dripped it into Pip's snoring, open mouth. He coughed and gurgled in his sleep.

"Pip!" I barked. "Awake!"

The sleeping cherub – and he would look like one

were a human's idea of a cherub whitish blue and buglike – roused shakily. He turned half-closed eyes toward Tamara by way of welcome. She did not school her face. Pip sat up groggily for explanation.

"Cupid," I redirected. "We must make this permanent." Turning to Pip, I added, "Pip, face Cupid."

Pip swiveled toward his left, yawning, to face Cupid, whose eyes turned stormy. I held the crown in front of Pip.

"Cupid," I commanded. "Fire at will."

"I'd love to." He drew an arrow in a flash.

Pip squeaked and teetered upward. I extended my arm with crown in hand to follow him. Pip zigged, but Cupid's bow zagged, and I do believe that no being, mortal or everliving, could escape the shaft of the god of love. The arrow grazed the inside of the crown and bulleted through Pip's forearm.

"Waaah!" Pip cried, seizing his pierced limb to protect against life-threatening blood loss. There was no blood lost. Pip's divinely pierced skin closed up as soon as the arrow had passed and didn't even leave a mark. Pip swayed wildly, flittering this way and that, yet still advancing with the chariot, presumably to have a place to collapse in heroic death. "Cupid's killed me!" Pip wailed. "I'm dying! I'm so young!"

(Stagehands, forgive the tiresome task of shaking the Pip beanbag. I do understand that it must be nearly in tatters, but Pip really believed himself to be at death's door.)

Tamara crossed her arms at his hysterics and eyed him with increasing impatience.

"I was a good messenger!" Pip sobbed. "I deserved better!"

Tamara finally reached up and snagged his leg. He screamed and writhed to escape, but she yanked him down and grabbed hold of his pricked forearm.

"Pip." Her voice was strong and demanding.

He stilled.

"You are not dying. Cupid would not kill you."

I wasn't so sure of that, to be honest. Certainly at the beginning of this quest, it was a distinct possibility. And I might have helped. Or at least looked the other way.

"He shot you using the crown's power to disable Mercury's access to your unconscious mind. Mercury's been using you as a spy against us."

Pip's dismay was so immediate and profound, I almost felt sorry for him.

"Waaah! I'm a servant *of* the crown! Not a spy *against* it!"

(Sound Techs, the recordings of a crying baby or a caterwauling tomcat would play nicely here.)

Tamara rubbed her brow. Cupid rolled his eyes

my way.

"Pip, control yourself," Tamara insisted, exasperation in her voice. "We know you had no part in this. It was Mercury all along, and we have to figure out ....our next... move." Tamara lost herself in deliberation, and Cupid's curious eyes fell upon her.

I hooked Vulcan's crown back inside the chariot. We were skimming well above land now. Africa's Great Sand Sea rolled below us. Its desert dunes crimped along, making the earth's surface look like a table of bunched, yellow silk fabrics. The dunes' crests cast shadows, darkening and lengthening with the waning daylight. Apollo would soon stable his horses for the night.

"Oh, I was a fool," Tamara said in her moment of epiphany.

"Never!" I exclaimed in her defense before Cupid could.

"But I was, Bacchus. And you told us at the start!"

"Of course I did," I concurred. "I will always tell you everything."

I knew not what I had told her.

Cupid shook his head at me in possessive warning. The threat might have impinged me before, when we were both actively vying for the lady's attention, but, as I knew I'd already lost the battle, I chose to let him see that other suitors would have her hand were he to fail her. Let him eternally earn her precious affections.

Pip seemed impervious to the conversation around him. He continued rubbing his forearm, which surely didn't hurt.

"I should have seen then," Tamara said, fisting her hand in frustration.

"The plots of the gods are indiscernible," I said, acting along. "And as says Mr. Frost, 'Evil is stronger than passing time.'"

"Cupid, don't you see?" she asked, turning around to face her beau directly. "I got it all wrong. The Fates' warning wasn't about Vulcan but about Mercury."

Cupid slapped a hand to his forehead, understanding washing over him in the same delicious moment.

Tamara continued. "Morta had said, 'To trade and deal is his heart's desire.' That's Mercury, all the way. He's the god of business and commerce. 'The still and slumbering night to mire.' By interrupting people's dreams 'cause he's the god of dreams and the unconscious. 'With dishonesty and covetous ire.' So he's making things appear unlike how they really are because he's jealous of something and angry about it. 'Turning favor toward himself, the liar.' So he's getting people on his side by lying." She put a finger to her temple and thought. "Like Triton," she said with certainty. "Triton was talking about family lines and ascension plans. So Mercury's got people against you as royalty. Maybe. But what ascension plans? You already are a god. So what's to ascend to? What are they thinking?

Bacchus, you said you saw Mercury lurking around Jupiter. Does he have Jupiter against Cupid, too? Is that what this mission was? A way to endanger Cupid? But why?"

Cupid stared at her mute as she thought aloud the very plot that I'd described when I first met her. Somewhat. Well, I'd hinted at it.

"And then Morta turned the warning to me," Tamara went on. "She'd said, 'You! Beware of your tenuous position.' Is my position tenuous, Cupid?"

He shook his head faster than a wet dog drying off.

"My tenuous position," she repeated quietly.

"The Fates are impossible to understand," Cupid said.

Tamara frowned.

"But I'll never ignore them again," he quickly assured her.

"What position does Morta mean? I hold no position."

I heard Cupid's reluctant thoughts. *If we married, you certainly would.* He spoke nothing.

She continued, "'A contender's undermining mission may steal your courter, your swain some night.' I'd thought it was Vulcan who would steal my swain, my boyfriend, away from me. And he almost did! But I think now Morta meant Mercury would take you away, Cupid, because Mercury's got it in Triton's head to want to kill you."

She paused, contemplating the rest.

Cupid paused, absorbing the revelation.

Pip paused, understanding finally that he would survive Cupid's arrow and thus coming to the conclusion that he really ought to listen to what was going on around him.

I did not pause. The Fates' final line was the tour de force.

"Go on, Tamara," I urged her.

"'Tis stolen love,'" Tamara answered. "'And vengeance right.' I had thought the 'stolen love' was Venus', stolen from Vulcan by Mars. Or maybe my love for Cupid, stolen by Vulcan being vengeful. But now I see who tried to steal my love away from me."

Tamara tensed.

Cupid took a step back and bumped into the inside wall of the chariot.

Pip looked from actor to actor.

My grin was smug.

"Like hell I'm letting Mercury get away with this," she announced.

All three panthers roared in healthy approval.

I nodded in satisfaction.

Act III begins.

Chapter 25

CHANGING PERSONAS

D usk deepened as we soared over the Indian Ocean, allowing us easy and unmolested travel. Our eyes grew accustomed to the darkness of the open sea. When we felt the air shift around us, we knew we'd reached Western Australia. It wasn't long before the twinkling lights of cities beckoned us to the more populous, eastern side of the island-continent and then finally to Sydney's famed Opera House.

I nearly wept with joy. This glorious building with its exquisite roof lit Sydney Harbor like a polished necklace centerpiece. The roof's cascading white shells, unequaled in beauty and form, are unmistakable. The site's celebrity, unquestioned. The House stands as an applauded symbol of the world's finest performances and expression. Even its interior, with sweeping glass accents and plush, inviting, red seats, calls to my sense of artistry as much as wine calls to my passion.

As we approached, I saw that the roof's classic white shells, always lit for nighttime splendor, were tonight bathed in soft pink, their hue as delicate as rose quartz crystal, and far more enchanting than the city lights beyond. Their reflection fragmented in the lapping waves below.

I was home. Among the cognoscenti.

Pip fluttered forward to hover between my head and Tamara's. He and Cupid had been silent for some time.

"I should fly ahead to announce your arrival at court," Pip suggested solemnly. "It's the custom, you know."

Of course I knew, but I wasn't at all convinced that we should announce ourselves at all – or even arrive in a recognizable fashion. I sensed an ambush.

"Wait, Pip," Cupid answered. "Bacchus, can you pull out *any* of the items cast on your chariot?"

I smiled with pride, both because, yes, I'd had the forethought to ask Vulcan for that little dido, but also because I had in fact chosen the right actor. Cupid indeed could be a leader – if the moment to lead should arise.

"Yes, Cupid. I can withdraw from its confines everything cast in my chariot," I answered smoothly. "I can also add to the casting as needed."

"Well, then," he said happily. "It's time to play dress up. I'll create some cover."

And with that simple statement, Cupid did something I'd normally very much protest. He thrust his arm forward and drew from the atmosphere a swirling cloud cover so large and thick that it encircled the entire Opera House like the cigarette smoke ring blown by a Titan. The impenetrable hoop effectively shrouded our approach but also hid that magnificent sanctum from the world. The arts should never be hidden.

My cats ignored the travesty before them and

dipped into the haze. They slowed to hover. I reached over the side of our ride and pulled from its silver walls an entire wardrobe of kingly ermine cloaks, fitted princely short jackets and knee breeches, sixteenth-century Venetian long gowns, and eighteenth-century French rococo frocks with their obligatory pannier hoops. I handed the piles over and simply pointed to the chariot's side to show my assortments of masks from which to choose. Tamara and Pip leaned over and gasped. I have a penchant for collecting masks; my collection is quite startling.

Everyone chose something they fancied and flitted out of sight to change behind the thick curtain of cloud surrounding us. I wondered why Cupid bothered. We'd all seen him naked not 24 hours earlier. Ah, feigned modesty. Only slight hypocrisy, I suppose.

I noticed that Tamara chose a deep purple satin gown with elaborate black embroidery. The gown's giant, layered hoop skirt connected to a much trimmer, fitted bodice. Its pagoda sleeves fit tightly from shoulder to elbow before flaring flamboyantly in an explosion of lace and ribbon. The whole thing swayed and swished delightfully in her arms even before she'd graced it with her form. I was delighted to see a tall powdered wig teetering on top of the mass of fabric in her arms. Some of the wig's tresses had been swirled into nests to hold tiny, glass figures of birds of paradise. To see Tamara in such bygone finery would be a great delight.

I changed (right in my chariot) into a bright blue long jacket with lighter blue breeches, cream-colored hose, and flat, grey, buckled shoes. My mask was large and loud, however: shiny and black with a very long, sharply-pointed, grey beak, fanned by brown-and-white-striped turkey feathers. Perfection. I waited but a moment for my companions.

Pip popped out of the white world surrounding us sporting an outfit that I recognized immediately from our rendition of *Raggedy Ann and Andy*. He wore a red, white, and blue sailor suit spiffed up with a floppy, black bow tie and light brown chukkas shoes. He topped it with a red yarn wig and a blue sailor's hat featuring a wide, white rim. The ensemble wasn't truly appropriate for a masquerade ball, but the rag doll's clothes were probably the only ones that fit him. I pulled a porcelain version of the doll out of my chariot's casting and handed Pip its detachable face.

"Your mask," I offered. Pip grinned widely. I suddenly wished we had a violinist to follow us. Nothing would add to the creepiness of a floating porcelain doll like the off-key scratching of a foreshadowing violin.

(Stagehands, at last you may replace the tattered bean bag Pip with a new Raggedy Andy doll. I imagine the old Pip is hanging by a thread anyway. Employ a good flick of the wrist to be done with it.)

Cupid emerged from the mist next, wearing a white, flowing blouse and trunk hose. The puffy shorts featured gold panels that I knew would sparkle when hit by the light just right. I decided not to tell him. He wore a matching gold mask and chose to accent the ensemble with ruffled, plum-colored man heels. I surmised that Cupid's foray into conservative style was over. And so I wolf whistled.

"Watch it, turkey. I'll pluck out more than your feathers."

I had no idea what that meant.

A movement out of the corner of our eyes had us turn in time to see Tamara emerge from the fog, draped in the color of royalty and shaming all who'd dared wear the hue before her. She was the very symbol of elegance and finery. Her grey and white powdered wig brought out the warmth of her darker skin. She'd chosen a blood-red half mask on a stick with a giant, wispy black plume bursting straight up from its side. She was a vision so welcome that even if she herself were *The Mask of the Red Death*, I would willingly succumb.

Cupid coughed in response to this vision. In fairness, he was as shocked as I, but I had the benefit of his cough to snap me out of it.

"You look ravishing, my dear," I said.

"Thank you," she answered simply.

"Gorgeous," Cupid added quickly.

"Thank you, too," she answered. "We're all looking swanky, aren't we?"

I was suddenly and strongly reminded of the purpose of masquerade balls, to provide a night of risk and perhaps anonymous debauchery within otherwise strict society. This was another moral hypocrisy, but one that eventually came to its logical conclusion. Any student of history can tell you that anonymity breeds ferocity. Such was the case for Gustav III of Sweden, assassinated at his own ball by masked noblemen avenging his revolution's reforms. When it comes to drama, royal courts need no help from me. I worried whether tonight's ball might end in a similar manner.

"I'm ready," Tamara said, not possibly understanding what we were getting ourselves into. I didn't either.

As such, I unhooked Vulcan's crown from inside my chariot, leaned over the side, and pushed it into the transport's casting. The silver softened and rippled as my hand pushed in, then turned transparent, very much like water. I could easily see the entire scene within to reach just where I wanted to place the crown: around a circular cameo frame hanging near a coat rack. It was effectively invisible.

With my hand still groping within the silver scene, I reached into a real (and stolen) pirate's chest (That's another story.) and pulled out the golden crown of Gorm the Old. Gorm was the first king of Denmark, itself

Europe's oldest continuous monarchy, and he built the Jelling Stones (not Jellystone – although both places are famous – ha!).

Old Gorm always loved our talks and appreciated the fine arts enough to donate his tenth century crown, worth a fortune. (I have so many treasures; how else do you suppose I could fund my performances?) Gormy's impressive skull topper has since graced the head of my every King Lear. The crown has heft and presence, with its roughly engraved golden circlet, yet it tolerates no pretentious arches for jewels or height. This was a crown for a more level-headed monarch. No one would doubt it to be Vulcan's.

"Cupid, I suggest you wear this." I handed it over. "Let all in attendance see it and make whatever assumptions they will, if they make any at all. We don't know how many people Mercury's influenced."

Cupid nodded and fitted the crown regally upon his curlicued head.

He was about to remount the chariot when a sing-song chant carried over the mist, arresting us where we stood. The chant was high-pitched and childlike. We looked toward its source and watched the mist separate as if the song itself demanded it. As the mist blew away, we found ourselves quite near three little girls, who turned their chant into a humming rhythm. Their knee-length, pink dresses were so ruffly that I wondered if they had just popped out of a ball of cotton candy. The girls were young, sixish, I'd say, and Latina, with pale skin, straight brown hair, and huge eyes that stared relentlessly. Two girls stood side by side, holding hands, while the third jumped rope, her ruffles bouncing to the hummed beat.

I'd barely taken in this scene when Tamara rushed over to the eerie triplets and curtsied deeply. Her own dress puffed as she dipped. I focused on one girl in particular, the athlete of this sinister apparition, and noticed that she hopped over the thread of life. Aaaah, Morta, the Fate who cuts the thread of life, essentially murdering mortals every day. (And people have a problem with something as trivial as my drinking.)

The hand-holders used their free hands to point toward the building, then at me. In unison the three little ghouls turned their hum to a jumping song, pinning me with their gaze. Their scrutiny unnerved me, and I had the strongest urge to flee.

> They sang:
> "*Merrymaking, wine, good cheer,*
> *Are found within this belvedere.*
> *But 'tis a mere veneer, a sphere*
> *Of fear drawn near.*
> *Give austere ear!*
> *The stage 'tis not real life, good lord,*
> *Not free from danger nor the sword.*

And thoughts hissed 'round do oft congeal.
The king's worst foe hath set his seal.
'Tis time to act and not to play.
This scene must end ere dawn's new day."

(The Fates turned their gaze to Cupid. Light Crew, swivel the spotlight.)

Contrast love, no start, no end.
Contrast hearts, its goal to mend.

(Now to Tamara, and soften the glare.)

To set minds right forevermore,
Consider what the tool is for.
Tormented minds can bend and sway,
And no force doth keep dreams at bay.
But, ah, a muzzled dog shan't bite
Nor find false friends to aid his fight.
This dog, his ruff as rough can be,
Yet cannot fight a ruff from thee.

(The Fates paused dramatically as if they'd finished but then turned their gaze to Pip, I assume to prevent him from feeling left out. Stagehands, keep the new Pip doll absolutely still as an apt portrayal of the terror that froze him.)

Your talent new, your pluck recovered,
Best to blend until discovered.

A princess calls for aid in time
To free a master from the crime."

The Fates silenced. Morta kept time with her hops.

Pip looked at Cupid and whispered, "Did they just call me a princess?"

The fog began to cloak the Fates once more. Tamara raised her face and whispered, "Thank you."

"Mesdames," I called, but the crones-turned-lassies returned to the mist. Well, they understand drama better than nearly anyone. They'd said their lines and were now letting them sink in. Their tale was told.

"I get it," Tamara said, rising and turning back to the chariot.

"You get it?" Cupid asked, incredulous.

She nodded before asking me, "Bacchus, do you have paper here?"

"On your command," I replied and pulled from the chariot's side a small scroll, goose quill, and brass inkwell.

Tamara took the writing tools from my out-stretched hand and scribbled away. After a moment, she waved to Pip, who was already hovering over.

"Pip, would you please get this to Tyrone, Jarel, Tommy, and Cornelius?"

I knew the names from her previous adventure. Tyrone was Cupid's former chauffeur – and spy after his master's banishment. Jarel led Cupid to the rest of them and discovered Pluto's plot. Her protective friend Tommy had taken over the task of providing redeemable work for those unfortunate Fallen Angels who hadn't sided with Cupid during the last rebellion; those angels were hoping to earn their way back into Jupiter's good graces. Her love angel friend Cornelius now manned the Hit List, the daily roll call of unsuspecting humans to be lovified; the more names The Fallen could hit, the more of them might be redeemed.

Pip didn't hesitate to toss the scroll into the air, wipe a hand under his armpit, and fling the glittering dust he'd withdrawn from that curious nook onto the parchment. The scroll disappeared in an instant.

"What is going on?" Cupid demanded. "What The Fates said, what am I supposed to contrast?"

"Your *lack* of understanding to Tamara's *skill* at it," I jabbed. My, I am a logophile.

Cupid's jaw clenched. I heard a storm of angry thoughts emanating from him, along with some calculating ones. I supposed I'd have to enjoy these final dips into his psyche.

"We continue with the plan," she answered.

"What plan?" he asked. The poor, oblivious thing.

(Music Tech, resist the urge to play circus music.)

"You've known since the moment we saw the effects of the crown, Cupid," Tamara answered.

I would have bet my own crown that he didn't.

"Pip," Tamara called, turning toward him again. "The Fates said it was best that you blend until discovered. You should be hidden. Can you do silver?"

It took Pip a moment to understand the question, but he soon puffed out his puny chest and said, "I believe I can."

"Then make like my favorite crayon."

"Ho-o-o-o-o-w," Cupid asked, flummoxed, "do you figure that'll make him hidden? It'll draw *more* attention to him. He'll look like a cheap, hyperactive ornament."

Pip frowned before allowing his eyes to light with the pride of discovery. "Oh, I'm going to hide against the chariot, aren't I, Miss Tamara?"

"Yes, Pip," she replied and petted him gingerly on the head like one might a child. "At the right moment, I'll call for you." She turned her face toward me. "Bacchus?"

"Yes, I can keep the surface soft for him," I answered, guessing her unspoken question. I placed my entire hand on the silver casting. My handprint biometrics would keep it "open" for some time now. Pip settled on the silver's surface, holding on to its framed edge. Then he shimmied to silver and blended in with the relief as if he were a part of it for centuries: a silver, buglike, Raggedy-Andy-esque cherub. Because that blends in great.

"Oh, I get it!" Cupid announced, and I heard him formulate an entire plan in his mind. "But this is going to require some theater."

"That it will," I said. "It's time to step through the looking glass."

"The Fates said, 'Eer dawn's new day,'" Tamara warned. "We don't have much time. Let's go."

She settled in to the chariot beside me. The panthers started moving. And so Cupid had no choice but to rush in.

Chapter 26

THE PLAY'S THE THING

My panthers landed on the sidewalk promenade alongside the Opera House. Once they settled the chariot, they shook loose their reins and ran to its side to form an intimidating security detail before us.

I appreciated their concern but knew their presence would betray us. Sure enough, not a second passed before a beautifully plumed rooster popped out of a potted plant and began frantically flapping its feathers. The cockerel, I knew, was Mercury's pet and spy, tasked tonight, no doubt, to crow our arrival.

I pointed. My cats sprinted. The clumsy cock tussled and squawked but was soon crushed in my alpha cat's jaws.

"Must your pets kill everyone else's?" Cupid asked incredulously as the pard trotted back with the cock-a-doodle hanging from its teeth.

"Be glad it did." I turned and heartily slapped my alpha's back. "Now prowl, my friends. Find the remaining birds. Use the mist and shadows."

Tamara watched them stalk away until the fog swallowed them. "What if we need them?" she asked with a hint of worry.

"Then they'll come."

We looked further down the sidewalk to our left, found no more roosters, and donned our masks to approach. Every door to the Opera House hung open. However, the party and dancers frolicked outdoors, farther down the path. And what a sight they made.

The shifting mass of masked deities swirled in their gowns and finery of old as if their charade were no farce of time, as if their make-believe could break the shackles of caste and claim. God and angel, privileged and working class, all hid behind their mask such that none could identify the other, which was the point for the nonce. We gods may eclipse humans in splendor, but do not doubt that we occasionally pine for mortality, the better to appreciate the resplendence of a rare, fleeting moment in a finite life, free of everlasting repercussion.

These beautiful people waltzed in formal lines and weaved in careful choreography. And while the ball was meant to honor Jupiter's wedding anniversary, I couldn't help but notice that most of the attendees were either single or pretending to be so, judging by the way they eyed one another. There appeared to be less than a dozen bona fide couples; they were off in groups, away from the hubbub of the dance floor.

I knew how these events degraded throughout the night. Within a few hours, the more cultured and cumbersome attire would be shed – but never the masks – and the songs would morph from waltz to club.

Looking beyond the guests, I noticed a curtained area far back, abutting the building itself. Through its thin veiling, I could just make out five figures. Two were the silhouettes of birds on a thick perch: Jupiter's eagle and Juno's peacock, no doubt. How they contrasted! The other three figures were celestials: one thin, standing beside the two others, they being, I gathered, the royals. The latter two sat stiff-backed upon small chairs with arched backs through which weak streaks of light shone through. I suspected the thrones were wicker. How artsy – and convenient for travel.

A long and laden buffet table spread between the royal tent and the dance floor. I smiled. Food is always a good idea.

Cupid stepped onto the plaza beside me. I heard him counting the attendees and calculating, *Too many people; too many angles.*

"In theatre," I whispered by way of reassurance, "the size of the audience is of no concern. The actor compels viewers to see the hero as they see themselves, as the star of their own story. It's the theatre of the mind. Now, someone who's spent too much time in the mind, in villainy, might resent a loss of spotlight."

"The problem here, Bacchus," Cupid whispered back, "is that, in this public's eyes, the villain *is* the hero."

"Then you must correct them, as champion of my tale."

Cupid breathed in deeply before turning to face Tamara. He took her right hand in his left, placed his right hand on her hip, and swung her forward onto the dance floor. The revelers ahead parted as they would for any dancer. No one seemed to take particular notice of the new couple, she clutching the stick of her red mask up to her face, he wearing his elastic-backed golden one.

As Cupid and Tamara waltzed toward the royals, I grabbed the nearest person who wasn't part of a couple. It turned out to be a waiter, about a half foot taller than me, dark and handsome, whose serving tray I snatched from his hand to plop onto a table. Before he knew what I was doing, I had him waltzing along with me.

Oh, gods, Cupid thought.

I am who I am.

We spun and chasséd through the throng, hoping to remain undetected before reaching the royal shelter. Every twirl brought a new flash of color. Every spin drew a new swish of chiffon or crinkle of taffeta. Every moment invited its own romance. My partner let me lead.

When we reached the buffet table at the head of the alfresco ballroom, Cupid stopped and bowed his thanks to Tamara. The gentlemanly deed perfectly matched the loving thoughts I heard from him since the moment he took her into his arms. He adored that woman. I certainly hoped he told her often.

Tamara smiled and brought down her mask.

Cupid lifted his own. The disguises had done their job cloaking us through the crowd. Cupid turned toward the tent and locked eyes with Jupiter's executive assistant, who was standing beside it.

Habandash, that slightly portly and definitely dowdy heavenly helper, gasped and ran a hand over his dark brown, heavily slicked hair, styled in its usual comb-over. He wore a tuxedo a size too small and thus scurried forward with careful restraint. Poor Habandash. He was the one unpleasantly tasked a few months ago with stripping Cupid of his title. Cupid's thoughts weren't hostile toward him, however. He knew that Habandash acted out of obligation.

I reached Cupid and Tamara at the same time as Habandash. I released my partner with a wink, and his parting smile told me I still had it.

"Cupid. Tamara," Habandash whispered urgently.

Cupid put up a hand. "Announce us only to him. No one else."

Habandash held Cupid's eyes a moment before turning toward the royal tent and disappearing inside. It was but a moment before the larger backlit shadow got to its feet.

Jupiter stormed out of his gauzy tabernacle, looking every bit as tall, regal, and sculpted as ever. His shockingly blue eyes sparked with anger, outshining the diamonds on his deep blue robes. His appearance was accompanied by a chill breeze that swept away Cupid's fog. **(Stagehands, a fan offstage, if you please.)** He strode to the buffet table and stopped on the side opposite us. His eagle soared through the tent opening to land at his feet.

As the cloud departed, Jupiter's sister/wife/regina, Juno, emerged from the tent along with her pet peacock. Her whole manner – her expression, her posture, her attire – was vexation veiled in propriety.

Tonight she wore long, grey robes, speckled white like sun-bleached concrete, with a blood red sash across her waist, which I imagined to look threatening to any of her husband's secret lovers. Juno's once strawberry blonde hair had gone nearly all silver, and her short curls shot in all directions as if she'd been buffeted by a windstorm – only, she always looked that way, so I knew Jupiter's wind-swept entrance had absolutely nothing to do with it. She kept as youthful an appearance as possible by drawing upswept lines on her upper eyelids (crinkly as those lines became on such a wrinkled canvas). She normally carried a deeply angry countenance as she spent the bulk of her time chasing her wayward husband and punishing his conquests even as she wasted her youthful beauty on him and lavished him with unwarranted affection. Her actions made sense, given who she was. The protector of the state and goddess of marriage would of course work hard to preserve her own, even if the effort was wholly one-sided. Tonight, however, she looked unsure of herself, even troubled. Well, you can imagine *her* family drama.

Behind her, out skunked Mercury, wearing billowing red robes, following his big beak of a nose and shifting those beady eyes, which were at the moment trained on the back of Jupiter's head.

Cupid and I nodded to the royals in deference; Tamara curtsied deeply. "Your Majesties," we addressed in unison.

Jupiter looked back slightly over his shoulder to a doorway leading into the Opera House. Crammed just inside was the royal orchestra, which, at his glare, stopped playing. The dancers outside rolled to a halt. Seeing their royal host, everyone bowed or curtsied before rising again to witness... whatever. I guessed that this was the first time Jupiter had shown himself tonight.

The ground shook slightly, and the crowd no doubt believed Jupiter's sudden appearance had prompted it. They showed us no hostility, however. Perhaps Mercury only bothered accosting the upper crust.

"I summoned you two days ago," Jupiter boomed, "along with my assistant's First Messenger. Neither of you responded. You've ignored my royal command."

Jupiter's eagle spread his wings menacingly and batted them twice before returning them to rest.

The guests shivered in anticipation. I've noticed over the years that confrontation feeds *their* thirst for drama as much as mine. Mind you, *this* is a thirst for which no one faults me; it's my thirst for *wine* to which they object. Incidentally, I noticed the drink flowing freely here tonight.

"Pip is indeed missing, Sire," Habandash confirmed, regret etched in his sullen eyes. I wondered if Pip could hear all this back at the chariot. I hoped he wouldn't show himself.

I lifted my chin and offered in the friendliest but loudest of tones, "Pip did relay a confidential message, more than just a summoning. Would you like the message kept privy, sire, or would you prefer we discuss it here freely, among your guests?"

The crowd gasped. I admit that it was dangerously bold of me to demand a private audience when in truth Jupiter could simply dispatch us with a word. But *I* know something most others don't: the king loves a good show. The throne room gets awfully dull. Thus, his excursions. Thus, his affairs. Thus the *masked* ball.

Cupid openly adjusted the decoy crown upon his head. Jupiter made no sign of recognition, but Mercury did. He tensed and looked around for his spies and pets, no doubt expecting an earlier alert. Alas, there were no birds to be found; I was sure my cats found them delicious.

Mercury narrowed his eyes and hurried forward to stand beside his lord. Juno's mouth gaped at what was an insolent move by anyone's standards. Even close advisors are meant to stay back, but perhaps such rules of gentility do not apply to enchanters controlling their king. Whispers hissed through the crowd.

Habandash took a single step forward as well but was stopped from advancing farther when Mercury raised his hand. Clearly Jupiter's long-time, right-hand man had been ousted as the favorite. (Strings, a sudden trill, if you please to mark Mercury's plague of influence.)

I wondered for a moment why the god of trade hadn't tried to conquer Habandash – until I saw the god glance over his shoulder and ooze a sly smile his way. *Ah*, I understood. Mercury enjoyed torturing the butler, as it were, by controlling the master of the house. What guile!

Mercury looked to Cupid and said smoothly, "That crown looks burdensome." He rolled up the sleeves of his enormous red robe to offer both hands as a depository. "Perhaps you'd like it kept in safekeeping – until the end of the ball. I'd be happy to hold it for you."

"Ohoho, no," Cupid replied before turning to Jupiter. "This crown, Grandfather, may save the kingdom."

Mercury turned to watch the king's reaction.

Jupiter gazed curiously at the ancient circlet that couldn't compare to the grandeur of his own crown. His Majesty's royal cap bore so many colored jewels that one had to wonder how his spine bore the weight. By the king's disdaining look, he judged Cupid's crown as worthless.

"Save the kingdom? How so?" Jupiter asked. "I

must warn you, Cupid, that I've heard rumblings against you. There are *some* among us," he said with a meaningful pause, "that believe you to be upsetting the order of things, creating upheaval with gods of land and sea and sky alike. Perhaps hoping to take what is not yours. This is why I summoned you."

Mercury smiled at the beginnings of this public squabble. Such enmity could only prove political instability.

The ground trembled again ever so slightly. Once more, the crowd took it as Jupiter's agitation. He made no move to disavow them of this conclusion, but Tamara turned her head ever so slightly in the hopes of catching my eye. I nodded a warning. Juno's peacock scratched the earth.

"It's not me causing quakes and making waves, Grandfather," answered Cupid quite loudly. He was right to raise his volume; patrons from the pit to the very top of the mezzanine must hear the actors' lines. "But we've conquered that Vulcan, you and me together, and we were right to do it, too!" Cupid ripped the crown off his head and held it high for all to see.

Mercury stiffened as the crown was revealed to the crowd, perhaps its secret to be made public.

"Imagine a god creating a crown as a weapon!" Cupid went on.

Juno put a startled hand to her heart; she'd hate talk of Vulcan's weaponry. She looked around as if expecting another throne to sneak up on its tiptoes.

The crowd broke into urgent murmurs.

"Vulcan's crown?" asked Jupiter, his tolerance waning. "What do you mean by this?"

"Just that Vulcan is indeed the bright yet deviant fellow you expected him to be, Grandfather!" Cupid practically bellowed. "You were right. The fire god created this ingenious crown to break into people's minds. He could bend their will, control them with this. No other god has ever held such power."

Mercury seethed.

Cupid went on, "This crown is how Vulcan got Triton on his side to fight us, Grandfather. Vulcan is the cleverest of us all!"

Jupiter's guests gasped and covered their mouths and overacted, far beyond the pale. (Actors, emulate this. Go nuts. Act away. It's what you've always dreamed of.) (Were I myself the stage manager, I would certainly have extended the giant hook to yank Cupid offstage. No one, not even a god, should tell the king of the gods that another god is cleverer than he. But I knew the plot, and the other gods did not.)

I leaned slightly toward Jupiter, who was indeed confounded, and whispered loud enough for Mercury to hear, "Pip relayed your command that we secure Vulcan's crown, and just in time or who knows what that all-time genius might have accomplished."

Mercury's eyes flared in anger.

Jupiter looked at me as if I might grow antlers.

"I would not seek more trouble with my son Vulcan," Jupiter stated seriously. "We have peace between us now."

"Oh, but you were right to suspect him!" Cupid shouted. "Even Mercury here must admit the brilliance of Vulcan's plot! No doubt Vulcan meant to turn the gods against me, then turn them against other gods in turn, until no one was left to defend one another. How easy it would be to claim the kingdom when no one was left but him!"

('When no one was left but *he*,' I refrained from correcting.)

Mercury looked ready to burst with rage.

"Imagine if Vulcan had gotten further in his plan, Grandfather. Of course, no one else could do it. No one else is smart enough or daring enough to try such a dastardly plan!"

"It's a simple plan," Mercury broke in, "if you think about it."

"Ha! You didn't!" Cupid urged. "Not a robust enough brain in ya'."

"Not robust enough!" Mercury scoffed. "I'm the god of commerce. I can plot!"

The ground shook. Everyone looked to their feet, frightened. I saw a small fissure open in the ground below me and a tendril of smoke escape it. I stepped blithely to the side should anyone need to see up through it.

He's here, Cupid thought. I looked up to see him return his attention to Mercury.

"Mmm, you're also the god of messages, right?" Cupid continued. "Well, get this message. Vulcan is a genius."

Mercury squeezed his lips shut. The tiny wings on his hat and sandals began to flutter.

My cats appeared at the table's faraway ends and prowled toward us, licking their chops at the heaping mounds of smoked salmon so near. They would not eat from this particular table without my go-ahead. Their eyes turned toward the eagle and peacock. I pursed my lips in warning, yet they leaned back onto their haunches, ready to spring.

Cupid goaded on, "You sound almost sorry, Mercury, that you couldn't come up with such a brilliant plan yourself! But no mere messenger god could take over a kingdom. You haven't got what it takes."

Mercury balled his hands in fists and shot up into the air over Jupiter. Juno and Habandash exchanged confused glances.

"You certainly can't be the heir!" he bellowed.

And with that, Tamara rended the air. "N-O-O-O-O-O-O-W!"

The spectators near her stepped away, confused.

Cupid and I whipped around to see Pip fly over the crowd like a bullet, flashing like mad. He soared over

Cupid's head and dropped between him and Jupiter. Cupid drew an arrow quick as a flash and aimed it at the king's heart.

"Protect His Majesty!" Habandash shouted and dived toward him.

Jupiter's eagle launched itself up to take the attack.

"I'm sorry, Grandfather," Cupid said, and he fired upon his king.

Chapter 27

THE AIM HERE IS TO AIM

Jupiter stumbled back – with an arrow in his heart – and fell into Juno's arms.

His majestic eagle crashed to the ground, feathers splintered, having been run through by Cupid's arrow.

Juno buckled under Jupiter's weight. Her peacock scurried to her side.

Mercury dropped beside them while Habandash scrambled over.

"You see, my king?" Mercury shouted, grabbing the king's chin and shaking it to see if he was still alive. Somehow I doubted Mercury was happy to see life still in him. "Cupid rebels against you."

Habandash slapped away Mercury's hand. Juno shifted Jupiter to one arm and used her free hand to rip the arrow away.

Mercury leapt into the air again and pointed at us, quite dramatically I might add. He commanded unseen guards, "Seize them!"

Pip disappeared with nary a pop. I wondered if he remained right there in front of us, highly camouflaged. Cupid grabbed Tamara's elbow and yanked her away from the dozen arms reaching toward them. The hands laid on me were quickly gored by my leaping cats. As the hands' owners screamed, I pointed to the table. Two of my panthers leapt onto it, roared mightily, and began tearing up the buffet. They swatted food onto the unsuspecting guests, leapt up and down, and created just the right amount of chaos. The beta panther charged through the crowd, slamming into whomever wasn't fast enough to flee.

I looked up to see Tamara and Cupid back to back, arrows trained on the dozen or so members of the Royal Security Force who'd burst onto the scene. She seemed to be saying something to him, but I couldn't hear.

"Mercury was right," said a feeble voice on the other side of the table. I looked to see the king righting himself. "Cupid was plotting. Riling Triton. Stealing from Vulcan. I see that my faith in him was misplaced."

"Was your faith misplaced, my lord?" I asked calmly. "Think back to what initially gave you faith and then what caused you to doubt it."

He stilled.

I added, "And who could make Pip think you ordered a heist?"

Our eyes met.

His eagle, unharmed, tested his massive wings.

A party guest screamed far back in the crowd. I looked in time to see her dodge a ham hock, no doubt slung by my faithful pets. She must have then seen a more frightening sight because she pointed to the bay and cried shrilly, "Look!" (I'm sure everyone not in immediate danger of panthers or flying food did indeed look. Incidentally, those are two of my favorite things.)

The bay's waters, normally so gentle, frothed with the mass surfacing of a splendid merbrigade. Male and female alike, hundreds of merfolk broke the surface and raised themselves high. Their hair glistened, slick as seaweed, dripping water onto their muscular torsos. Merfolk are magnificent from afar. Not so nice close up, though.

(Casting Director, hire the agency's most beautiful, toned beings. Makeup designer, paint upon them a green and grey pelt. Costume Designer, adorn them with seashell necklaces, weaved-seaweed bracelets, and shark-teeth piercings. These specimens of physicality are to pop up from the orchestra pit and brace themselves, stiff-armed, to the stage's edge. Let their magnificent torsos awe the audience while their mertails wave against the stage's skirt.)

Far behind the merfolk's front ranks, a new figure rose high above the water. This figure was the largest and fiercest of all, and one that I recognized far too well. Triton poised to let us landlubbers see him before he locked eyes with Cupid.

"See who arrives?" Mercury crowed. "Neptune's children won't allow such rebellion! And they'll be rewarded when authority changes hands."

I looked toward Jupiter. "Is authority changing hands?"

Jupiter looked confused. He shook as if to clear his head. "I had plans for Cupid. Faith in him. But then I felt Mercury should be heir. And I told him so."

"He's had far too much influence on you lately," Juno warned.

I looked up to see Mercury listening in. Farther up, Cupid was firing like a madman, and Tamara, having emptied her quiver, reached over her shoulder to take arrows from his. Some of the arrows caught in her powdered wig; anyone seeing it would think the wig had absorbed an attack. Cupid and Tamara fired solely to deflect the darts fired upon them by the Security Force; not once did the couple attack the guards themselves.

"I – you," Jupiter blustered to his queen. "You wanted Mercury to take over. And Habandash did, too. Everyone did."

By the apoplectic looks that crossed their faces, I'd say this was shocking news to them.

I looked up to see Mercury's reaction. Instead, I saw the light around us change. Beyond Cupid and Tamara, the stars in the sky suddenly obliterated. The sky itself shifted. A dark mass dropped down, and I realized it consisted of several hundreds figures. (Riggers, ready more wiring.) At the lead were four figures

I recognized abstractly as a result of their fame. A pudgy, white angel with a light brown afro and a pudgy, brown angel with a crop cut – these must be Cornelius, the Hit-List Keeper, and Tommy, Redeemer of The Fallen. Another angel next to them had a faded haircut and was highly muscular; that must be Jarel, the one Tamara said had gone off to train with Mars Senior. The final angel was very dark and boasted sleek, black wings – Tyrone, I believe, Cupid's former chauffeur.

Good ol' Tamara, I thought.

Cupid saw his friends charging in and the massive reinforcements in the sky behind them and threw his decoy crown their way.

Mercury shouted and shot its way. He, the fastest god of all, became but a red blur, his robe billowing all around him. He raced toward the crown, extended a hand, and got to within an inch of it when a blue cherub dressed as a rag doll appeared out of nowhere as if he'd crawled through a hole in space. Pip snagged the crown and popped out of existence, leaving Mercury, with his madly fluttering winged hat and sandals, to soar past empty handed.

(Actors, the audience will erupt in applause; keep on keeping on.)

Reappearing in nearly the same spot with prize in hand, Pip raised the decoy crown high and positioned Vulcan's real crown at its base. Then he glowed brighter than any star above.

(Sound Crew, activate the boom mics.)

Tommy, Cornelius, Tyrone, and Jarel shouted in unison. "FIR-R-R-R-R-R-E!"

The collective scrape of hundreds of arrows drawn from their quivers brought quivers to my soul. The thwoop of so many drawstrings stretched to their limit stretched the tension of my being. And the resounding thwacks of release released my resounding delight. I watched enthralled as a storm of arrows skimmed the crowns' inside and outside edges and rained down upon the unsuspecting crowd.

My panthers scattered. Jupiter's guests panicked.

(Crew, let me see pandemonium onstage. Party guests should be tripping over their suit coats and gowns, indeed tripping over one another to escape.)

"Fallen Angels, hit everyone!" Tamara shouted on high. "Earn back your rightful place!"

The Fallen dropped lower, the better to position themselves, and I saw hope radiate across their faces. They'd wrongly sided with Pluto mere weeks ago but had six months to prove a change of heart. Tonight, they would be unstoppable. What fun!

The Royal Security Force, defenders of king and realm, plummeted to protect their charges. They huddled the king and queen and draped their protective wings over them. The guards' concern and actions were admirable, but, really, none could defend Jupiter better than he himself.

(Crew, add still more extras to the crowd's outer edges. The stage should be tight with celestials, more arriving every minute, drawn from the interior of the Opera House to investigate the pandemonium. Once they perceive the riot they've entered, they too scramble for cover.)

"Triton!" Cupid bellowed, the golden panels in his puffy shorts sparkling spectacularly. He pointed down the sidewalk. "Don't let them escape!"

Escapees? I thought. *How thrilling!* I hopped onto the buffet table to better see the action. A torrent of arrows fell relentlessly on Jupiter's guests. Cellists ran, shielding themselves with their instruments. Some of the younger and sillier guests hoped to block arrows with upheld masks, imagining them to be impervious umbrellas, I suppose. Down the sidewalk they went.

Triton's merbrigade dived under the surface. The bay's water rose and fell in waves as the merfolk picked up speed. When they overpassed the land-bound sprinters, they swerved toward the sidewalk. The merfolk stopped and popped their heads out just as their giant wave crashed landside. Those celestials who weren't knocked to their feet were instead hit by a new wave of arrows, pelting down. Pip had followed the crowd, flashing brightly, and brought The Fallen with him.

I was quite shocked to have found not one hero for my tale, but three. I played the odds on Cupid when I sided with him at the start. I relied on reputation for Tamara. But I admit to expecting Pip to be a mere bit player. How wrong I was to have underestimated his grit! Imagine a lone archer firing darts in your direction while you stand still for it. Gutsy enough. To have hundreds fire at you? That's a remarkable level of daring.

Tommy, Cornelius, Jarel, and Tyrone led The Fallen over the final few guests who'd escaped their arrow deluge. They'd get them now. Those ball attendees who'd already been hit wandered about confused. I wondered if Pip hadn't upped the whammy on the crown's power by heating it to glow.

Not to be left out of the story's climax (and, thus, future retellings), I summoned my thyrsus just in case; it soared over from the chariot just as Mercury shouted, "You're ruining everything!"

I looked up to find him zipping in bursts around Cupid and Tamara, his winged hat and sandals buzzing wildly. He stopped for mere fractions of a second, holding his head in his hands over here and then shaking angry fists and reappearing over there. He was hard for me to even follow until he stopped cold with seemingly renewed determination. An evil smile split his face as he said, "Not every celestial is here. Your arrows can't have absorbed Vulcan's full power."

I admit to having thought the same thing.

"They'll wear off and be as nothing the moment the celestial sleep, which they eventually must! Sleep is my domain, and I'll rule again!" He looked toward Pip before returning to Cupid. "You and your outcasts can't hit everyone forever – and I'll make sure of it!" With that, Mercury shot off at breakneck speed toward the sea.

"P-i-i-i-i-p, m-o-o-o-o-ve!" Tamara shrieked.

Pip startled at the sight of a supersonic blur barreling down on him. He hugged the crowns to his chest and fled toward the merfolk. Cupid took off in pursuit.

Mercury evaded every mid-flight arrow that had been directed at the crowns. Cupid didn't have to; The Fallen stopped firing. Cupid took over, firing solely at Mercury.

Pip lowered to skim the water. Mercury followed, evading Cupid's missiles. His flapping red robes made him look like a wind-blown flame streaking across the water. Cupid dropped down as well, his plum-shoed toes hitting the water. I noted that it was the first time I'd ever seen him willingly approach the sea and the first time it didn't attack in return.

(Nonetheless, stagehands, make the cardboard waves bounce frantically.

This is an action scene after all!)

Pip zipped across the surface like a humming-bird. He collided with the crest of a rather large wave and bounced like a skipping stone.

Mercury too failed to give the wave enough distance and was slapped in the face by a meaty, green mertail. Mercury rolled and tumbled. Hands reached out of the water toward him. Mertails slapped across his back and legs. It was only Mercury's speed that prevented his being caught and drowned.

Pip swooped up before banking back toward land. Mercury followed just as Cupid crashed into the sea.

Pip looked back and must have seen his wingman gone and Mercury gaining ground because he yelped and dived near a panther in the crowd. My faithful pet leapt to snag Mercury but of course missed. The swiftest of gods was simply too swift.

A shout above me drew my eyes to Tamara. She'd thrown off her empty quiver, ditching her wig in the process, and was readying her bow like a baseball bat.

Pip raced toward her, Mercury hot on his wings. Cupid reappeared in the distance, panic in his eyes. He no longer fired.

I readied my thyrsus.

Pip was just about to soar past Tamara. He tried to boost his speed once more, but his tiny little buglike wings were no match for Mercury's godly ones. Mercury reached out.

Tamara swung her bow baseball style, I jumped and swung my thyrsus lacrosse style, and my two remaining panthers bounded, claws bared. No one hit the mark.

Mercury collided into Tamara and Pip. All three crashed through the tent and hit the building.

I landed awkwardly to pratfall onto the king. My cats skidded on the buffet and tumbled over the table's edges. Before any of us regained our footing, a member of the royal guard hoisted me up by my shirt collar. I tried to look over my shoulder to see if Tamara and Pip were alright, but the guard shook me, and so I wrapped my hands around his wrists, preparing for searing pain.

My skin shredded from forearm to hand as my ivy tattoos sprung to life, still tethered to my bleeding wrist, and stabbed the guard's arms. I concentrated with godly might that my tattoos would not cut his ulnar nerve.

He screamed. I screamed. Habandash screamed. (Sound Techs, give us the benefit of the doubt, please, and lower the pitch. It was a startling moment for all involved.)

The guard batted his wings to escape but remained tethered to my arms. His squirming only served to aggravate the agony of my burrowing vines. My cats would soon regain their footing. I didn't have time for this.

"Let go, and the vines will let go of you," I promised.

He released me, and my vines settled back onto

my arms, looking like fresh tattoos. I knew it'd be a few days before the fat, red tracings around them would settle. As the guard flew off and my cats bounded to my side, I chose not to linger on the fact that I'd saved that guard's life that day, thank you very much.

I whipped around. The tent's gauzy fabric jerked. A breeze shot forth, and Mercury whooped overhead with Vulcan's crown clenched in his hand.

I looked back to see the tent's fabric flutter to rest, revealing Tamara and Pip in a heap within.

Their eyes were closed, and they didn't move.

Chapter 28

CAPPED

N o!" Cupid shrilled. He was flying over the crowd, barreling my way.

I dashed over to place a shaking hand on them, but an explosion of noise made everyone crouch. Cupid stopped mid-air.

All eyes turned to the harbor. Triton stood high, atop his tail, arms raised. His imposing frame was immediately obscured by a wall of water that surged out of the harbor far above the Opera House. The wall leaned over and stretched itself over the top, above and around, encapsulating the building in a gigantic, impenetrable cap of seawater. Suddenly we were prisoners of whitecap waves, ominous shadows swimming within them. There a shark. There a killer whale. There electric eels sparking their warning.

I looked back to the harbor. So draining was this water wall that the merfolk rested in the shallows. Despite the Opera House's light bouncing off the inside face of the dome, I could just discern Triton, wagging a finger at Mercury. If the sea god could speak above water, I'm sure I'd hear him say, "Mercury, you go nowhere." Seawater rushed into the bay.

Jarel waved his arms at The Fallen, seemingly

mobilizing them, anticipating something.

Although all this happened in a mere flash, I couldn't waste another moment on it. I looked down and called out, "Tamara!" and shook her hard. She roused, startled, and shot to sitting. She took in the scene and immediately looked over at Pip. She gasped, and I right after.

Pip was grey. His eyes were half open. His chest didn't rise.

Tamara slapped her hands to her eyes.

Cupid landed hard beside us. He grabbed Tamara's shoulder, and she reached up to touch his hand.

Beyond him, I saw Mercury zipping along the dome, hunting for a weak spot, hounded by marine life. (Stagehands, lower a drape over the back half of the stage, one that is painted with waves and the scariest of dark shadows.)

"I'll work on Pip," I said to Cupid. "You must get that crown! The moment Vulcan falls asleep, Mercury will have him – along with every other living being!" (Except, perhaps, for the lunatics and we drinkers, whose minds would prove to be an impenetrable tangle even to him).

Cupid took off.

"Great gods," Jupiter said behind me.

I turned to see the king taking in the bedlam around him.

"Mercury got inside me," he said to no one in particular. "He got in my head. He tricked me."

"Of course he did," I replied testily. "As I indicated. But to quote The Bard, 'Uneasy lies the head that wears a crown.' When you laid down your head, the god of the unconscious broke in."

I couldn't talk more. Knowledge of revival skills is necessary in my line of work, to allow those foolish beings who mix wine with other stimulants a chance to learn from their mistake. But Pip wasn't a drunk or a fool. He'd become my teammate and, I realized with wonder, a bit of a friend. I tamped down my emotions. He needed me.

I began pumping firmly on his chest. Habandash scuttled closer, along with Jupiter and Juno. I counted thirty pumps before I noticed a pink splotch bloom just above his belly button. I lifted his rag-doll shirt and watched with curiosity as the splotch grew. It spread up his chest to his neck. Tamara cried out in relief. Habandash ran a hand down his face and coughed out a nervous laugh.

I massaged Pip like a baby. First his chest and belly. Then his arms. The color radiated. The royals let a worried sigh escape them.

Pip began moving under my hands, and so I snatched him up and dropped him right into Jupiter's arms. The king was shocked, but I was frankly annoyed. If he'd drink a bit more often, he could have prevented Mercury's brainwashing. I glanced over to see Tamara gazing at me in loving gratitude.

A swoop overhead broke the spell, and we looked up to see Cupid racing after Mercury, firing so many arrows, so quickly, that they blurred as much as Mercury.

"How dare you attack the king?!" Cupid shouted between blows.

"You won't be his heir!" Mercury shouted back.

"I never asked to be heir!" Cupid barked in reply. "And he's immortal! He'll rule forever!"

I shook my head in disbelief that Cupid could believe such nonsense. Had he not lost his own place recently? And all leaders must plan for eventualities.

I watched the chase, intrigued. Cupid simply could not keep up. He stopped to hover at mid-dome, above the crowd, firing wherever Mercury popped into sight or where he expected him to be. For his part, Mercury dodged every arrow, bolting from spot to spot, muttering to himself. At one point, he lingered at the dome's peak. I saw shadows fluttering outside of it. These were not sea creatures. These were celestials, outside the dome, home sleeping, no doubt, when Mercury called them nigh. I looked to Tamara, who registered the problem, too, but it seems we both registered it slower than Jarel.

The brawny angel charged across the inside edge of the dome, leading The Fallen behind him. He stopped, raised an arm, bellowed, "Charge!" and rushed the dome. He and The Fallen swam across, completely unmolested by the underwater killers. Any hole they made closed immediately behind them, and, when they burst out the other side, the beasts within protected their flank.

The resulting battle outside the dome could only be seen in flashes, clashes, and momentary crashes into the water.

I scrambled for my thyrsus and hopped up onto to the table. I'd seen plant life in the harbor's shallows. Maybe they could catch Mercury to end this all. I raised my arms, but a strafing attack of rapid-fire arrows came my way; I flopped to a crouch, and the strafe just missed me, pursuing Mercury as he rocketed over. Then, out of nowhere, a thunderbolt singed past.

When I untucked my head from under my arms, I caught sight of Tamara springing my way.

I raised a hand to my heart. Could it be?! Had I misread the signs? But, yes, yes, this was the story's climax, wherein the two tender lovers embrace. My moment at last! I offered her my most doting smile and held out a welcoming hand.

She scurried right by. Alas! I watched, newly wretched, as she climbed over the table and landed on all fours. She leaned her face to the ground and shouted something indiscernible into the fissure that had earlier emitted a steaming tendril. I couldn't hear in all the commotion.

The ground quaked again, and I felt land break

underfoot. I feared the Opera House might fall upon us.

Tamara popped up from her crawling position and flew my way. This time I knew better than to hope that the light through yonder window was breaking for me. She landed beside the newly enlightened king and dared – dared! – to not curtsy, to not wait for permission to speak, but to instead pull at his shoulder to whisper in his ear. No guard stopped her, proving discretion is the better part of valor.

The tiny fissure that had opened earlier beneath my feet, the one that had released a single tendril of steam, the one to which Tamara had flown, ripped open into a gaping chasm.

From it rose someone few hoped to ever see.

Chapter 29

PINNED

Heaving and swaying, a dragon clawed its way up the abyss. The beast was part metal, part lava, with a long neck and bulging shoulders behind which sat – oh, dear – Vulcan swinging his hammer. The beast (and here I speak of the dragon) was plated in gold and bronze and fashioned of gear work. Lava churned underneath the plates and even flowed outward to form thin wing membranes that stretched between metallic rod "bones." The dragon's impressive horns and spikes were made of pipes that spewed sparks or steam interchangeably. The whole contraption was gloriously steampunk. I loved it.

Oh, and Vulcan was his usual frightening self.

Vulcan waved his famous hammer overhead like a cowboy ready to lasso a steer. The hammer gave off red sparks, symbolic of rage or static cling, I couldn't know which. Vulcan howled before bellowing, "Who's gat me crown?!"

The terrified crowd, trapped with the god most feared to see angry, pointed at Mercury without hesitation.

The messenger god's winged hat and sandals shook with energy. Cupid huffed and puffed from on high, struggling to catch his breath.

Vulcan spurred his dragon with urgent kicks, and

the two gave chase. His dragon's wings took up much of the space within the enclosed area. The beast rose and dipped in pursuit. It spat fire whenever it caught a decent glimpse of Mercury, and the fleeing god's red robes sometimes made him look like a part of the spray, but Mercury always escaped the danger. He was just too fast.

Mercury caught on and started making hairpin turns at the dome. The third time he did, Vulcan's dragon banked too steeply. Vulcan slipped off. The crowd below scattered as Vulcan plummeted. He crashed onto the sidewalk, sending chunks of concrete flying in all directions and creating a rather impressive crater.

Cupid rocketed forward and hopped on the dragon's back.

Tamara rushed to Vulcan's side and tried to help him up.

"Get off me!" Vulcan chastised. "Don' ya know I've fallen from higher heights 'n this?!" He looked up and raised a fist to Cupid. "Get offa my dragon!"

Cupid ignored him and chased Mercury, firing arrows like a champion cavalryman, studying Mercury's flight pattern and beginning to anticipate his moves.

The shadows overhead crashed into the dome and distracted Mercury a mere moment, long enough for Cupid.

The love god spurred the dragon and dived off. The beast (and again here I speak of the dragon) hurtled forward and crashed into Mercury. They tumbled and rolled to the ground.

Cupid's arms were a blur as he fired dart after dart at the pair. An arrow caught Mercury's robe and pierced the dragon's metal plates. Then another. Then another. Within seconds, Mercury was pinned to the bucking beast's side, evoking a certain captain caught in a whale line. Call him Ishmael.

Something zoomed past me, and that sneaky little poltergeist, Pip, popped into existence beside Mercury and snatched the crown away. Pip's color changed again, and, before I could register it, he fluttered before Tamara, crown in hand.

Mercury thrashed. For once in all creation, the god of commerce could not negotiate his way out of this. His hostile takeover would be *no* takeover, but it *would* be intensely hostile.

The crowd stood rapt.

Tamara straightened up, drawing all eyes her way. "For trying to take my Cupid and for endangering my friends, for forcing my hand, Mercury, I take my revenge!" Tamara drew back Vulcan's crown like a discus and hurled it toward her tormentor.

(Riggers, slow the action of the wired, flying ring. Our enthralled audience will need time to take this all in.)

A streak of light burst through the sky as Jupiter launched his thunderbolt.

257

(Lighting Crew, strain the circuitry for one half second flaring every light we've got. Sound Techs, a spectacular crack of thunder, but do not damage hearing. The audience mustn't feel assaulted.)

The thunderbolt struck the crown in flight and broke it into a thousand, liquefied beads that hurtled toward Mercury. They wrapped themselves around his neck like a choker necklace, not so tight as to please his victims, but unable to come off without a beheading.

I felt a door slam in my head.

Chapter 30

THE RUFF

M ercury writhed, trying to dislodge the necklace. Cupid landed next to Tamara, and I heard none of his thoughts. I knew I never would again. The battle above stopped in an instant. Many of the shadows outside the water fled.

In a splash heard for miles, no doubt, the salt water dome and its creatures within retreated and slapped back into the bay. The stars above were visible once more.

"See what yer ill-gotten plottin's brung ya," Vulcan accused. "Tryin' ta get in my head fer years! An' now stealin' tha only thin' what stopped ya! Well, now ya'll have it ferever, ya' damned thief! Yu'll not get inta da minds'a da immortals no mo'!"

"Noooo!" Mercury begged, but his pleas soon died out. He stiffened as if electrified. All along the choker's edge, gobs of silver squirted outward to form needle-like fringes. I watched in horror as the fringes curled inward and burrowed their way into Mercury's skin. They sought his jugular and other veins, then coursed through his system. He suddenly glowed as his veins lit from within.

"You are guilty of treason!" Jupiter boomed. "Your thievery only grows. You invade my thoughts. You steal my will! You attempt to pilfer the kingdom itself!"

"I-I did it for the good of Olympus!" Mercury choked out. "You would have named Cupid as your successor! Don't you see? Olympus can't be led by Love! Love is an unpredictable emotion!"

He squirmed, the dragon shifted, and I was sure I heard something of Mercury's crack. He grimaced but continued his Machiavellian rant. "This kingdom isn't a lovesick fool's game of thrones! Olympus is a business." He was clearly recovering from the needling and doing some of his own. "Who better to assign as its CEO than me, the god of business? Me, who could rule as a king should."

Jupiter's light skin flared with electric current.

Vulcan grunted his impatience.

It was time to insert myself before anyone turned this adventure into a murder-not-so-mystery. "Ah, but Olympus is *not* a business," I corrected loudly. "It is a place of order and disorder, of powers and faith, of guidance and discord. You should know, Mercury, that by your attempt to infect my dreams, you left me no choice but to support a god whose very frivolity would love arts in all forms. None but Cupid for me."

"Argh!" the klepto huffed.

"Might I remind you," I went on, "that we are influenced by the company we keep. Perhaps your time spent with the cold, unfeeling dead – and Wall Street fat-cats, but I repeat myself – have caused you to forget the value of Love?"

"Cupid is the grandson of Juno alone," Mercury spat. "His father, Mars, is too warlike to offer a high position; he'd have us warring with each other and the mortals within an hour."

I couldn't argue.

Cupid looked ready to feed Mercury to my cats.

"The king's blood doesn't even run through his veins!" the disgraced god added.

"As it does yours? It runs equally through mine and the sun god's," I stated, eager to point out hypocrisy.

"Jupiter can't surrender the realm of the gods to a drunk," Mercury hissed. "And Apollo is too good at driving the sun to promote elsewhere."

I glared. Hard workers are so often kept from advancement, victims of their own success.

"So Vulcan was your biggest threat," I goaded, "as he enjoys the unusual benefit of both sides' regal blood."

Jupiter coughed a warning. Juno's eyes became slits at the voicing of her husband's notorious two-timing.

Mercury saw neither. He must not have thought before blurting, "Vulcan's a monster who begets more monsters."

The monster of whom he spoke snapped his fingers to disengage from the dragon the plates to which Mercury was attached. The plates, Mercury with them, drifted over to allow them to see face to face.

Mercury's eyes darted, looking for escape.

"Now it's metal what runs in yer precious veins alon' wit yer cherished royal blood," Vulcan retorted.

"A lesson for us all," I added. "Be careful what you wish for. You might instead get what you deserve."

Jupiter's eagle let loose a high-pitched cackle. (Disappointingly, a bald eagle's cry is nothing like what we entertainment producers depict onscreen and onstage. We impel our sound techs to dub over the call of a red-tailed hawk, which is far more robust. And that's one of the final insider tricks I'll divulge to you, reader. You're welcome.)

Juno's peacock screeched magnificently.

Jupiter raised his hands for silence and declared Mercury's punishment. "As it is your fate and a most humble task, you will continue to conduct the dreams of *mortals* and guide the newly dead to The Underworld. You will mediate between the realms. But you will never again taint the dreams of *immortals*. And your days in my court are over."

"But," Mercury wailed, "I'll be idled!"

I marveled at what some deemed to be punishments. I view idling as a wonderful thing, but I suppose it to be insufferable for the god of theft, commerce, and journeys.

"Hustle your trade elsewhere," Jupiter answered. "My new *lead* messenger is Pip."

Our cherubic hero gasped and exchanged a stunned glance with Tamara and Habandash.

"You won't be needing those anymore," Jupiter added. He curled a finger toward the humbled god's winged hat and sandals, and the curios pulled themselves away. They flew into Jupiter's hands, the king squeezed them in his fists, and out they popped Pip-sized. They flew of their own accord to their new master.

Pip whipped off his own shoes and hat, slipped on the new ones, and flew a loop faster than I could have come up with the idea.

"Mercury, my wayward son," Jupiter growled, "be gone until my anger ebbs." He raised a hand, shook electricity right out of the air, and produced a blinding bolt. Vulcan snapped his fingers to release the plates, and Jupiter hurled his bolt at the disgraced god. It caught Mercury and carried him out of sight.

"Thank you, my lord!" Pip gushed, but the king of the gods paid him no mind. He was now looking up.

Dropping out of the sky and landing right on the royal tent was Mars Senior in his enormous chariot. He leapt out of the transport and nodded to the queen.

"Hi, Mom," he sassed. "Jarel said there was something going on, so I went to Olympus, but no one was there. Then I remembered the ball. What'd I miss?"

Juno looked at her husband stonefaced. Vulcan chuffed aloud.

A murmur toward the sea drew our attention. The crowd parted, and Venus just stepped out of her clamshell, spumescent. She spun before I got a good look, and a magnificent, bright green, sparkling gown materialized on her flawless figure. I always eagerly anticipated seeing Venus, as does everyone, of course. I marveled at how she changed her look with each appearance. Sometimes she looked so womanly with long, wavy, brown hair and her speckled green/gold eyes. Other times she'd cut her hair into a boyish crop and complete the look with a gentleman's fashion. You know, tall, dark, and handsome.

"Arooooo!" Vulcan crowed. "There ya' be! Been lookin' fer ya fer hours!"

I turned back to study Mars, who barely contained his wolfish grin. I calculated the odds of he and Venus innocently arriving within seconds of each other.

Venus nodded at her husband but did not offer explanation. Instead, she floated gracefully through the crowd, past all the bowing and curtsying admirers, until she reached Tamara, who curtsied lower and more sincerely than any before her.

Venus put a hand under Tamara's chin to lift it. Then the goddess of love bent to kiss Tamara's cheek. They rose together.

"Thou hast moved me with thy devotion," Venus said. "I shan't forget."

Tamara smiled widely. It was a great honor. Of

course, anyone would smile after a kiss from Venus. Still, it was heartfelt, I would say, if not hypocritical as usual. I mean, really, the least loyal goddess in the kingdom values devotion? Need I say more?

"You showed up late to yet another battle," Cupid said with a hint of irritation.

She turned toward him, her expression cool. "Shall I repeat? E'er I doth show mineself afore battle, no battle doth ensue."

"Right," Cupid answered. "Better I nearly die than you stop a battle ahead of time."

Venus smiled, turned, and nodded to the royals around her. Then she raised a delicate, jeweled hand to her husband. His embarrassingly eager smile split his face from ear to ear. He reached out a gigantic hand, which engulfed her tiny one, and nodded for his dragon to approach. When the beast reached his side, Vulcan lifted his bride effortlessly onto the dragon and put his own foot on the beast's forepaw to hop aboard up front.

I tilted my head to catch Mars' expression. He looked away, but I had the feeling he wasn't unsatisfied.

Venus pointed skyward, Vulcan spurred his dragon, and the fantastical metal beast chugged and steamed and flapped away. The stones and debris that Vulcan had so dramatically torn through on his entrance rolled back to reseal the pavement. We were all lucky to have escaped so unharmed.

The Fallen fluttered down and landed among Jupiter's guests. Jarel, Tyrone, Tommy, and Cornelius landed nearest. They bowed, and the tubby one I knew to be Cornelius stepped forward and kneeled.

"Forgive us, Sire, for what must have looked like an attack," he said.

"The Fallen are reinstated," Jupiter announced without hesitation. "You have our deepest thanks, as do the merfolk beyond." Jupiter drew his arm overhead in a wide arc. "Thank you, Triton, you salty dog! This ball continues in our defenders' honor."

Juno's jaw dropped. "Our *anniversary* ball?!" she spat.

Cornelius stepped away. "Thank you, Your Majesties."

Jupiter raised his hand anew, this time toward Tamara. He said, "It's a fine collar you put on that dog. Mercury's muzzled now, and he shall stay that way."

Tamara smiled.

I sidled over to her and whispered, "'This dog, his ruff as rough can be, yet cannot fight a ruff from thee.' His ruff, his bark. Your ruff, the collar. Just as The Fates predicted. Well done."

"And now a short announcement to one and all before we resume the festivities," Jupiter stated simply. "We'll have no fuss or long pronouncement. Cupid is to be my heir – in the event of unexpected absence. I'll bear no discussion on it, for Cupid is the most powerful god of all."

Cupid blanched. Tamara raised an inquisitive brow. Everyone else froze in place, save Pip, Tyrone, Jarel, Tommy, and Cornelius, who whooped at the news.

The most powerful god of all? I mused.

I watched Triton nod his respects.

Strange, yet fascinating. As I contemplated, Juno slid to my side.

"How much did you have to do with this?" she asked.

"Me, Your Majesty?" I asked in innocence. "I know not what you mean."

The queen wrinkled her nose at me in plain disbelief. She looked me up and down before resigning herself to some level of eternal ignorance. Her parting words to me were familiar ones. "You really ought to cut down."

As far as I was concerned, her words were unbefitting. It was absolutely time for a toast and a waltz.

Chapter 31

DÉNOUEMENT

I think Jarel might be bored. He says Mars spends more time chasing after Venus than he does creating warfare," Tamara said as we danced. I was the fifth partner on her proverbial dance card. The order went: Cupid, Jupiter, Pip, Jarel, and then me. Mars Senior tried to push his way in, but Cupid dragged him back physically and forced him into Juno's arms. I heard something during the commotion about honoring your mother.

"Well, a rest is a necessity between wars," I advised, "if for no other reason than to allow time to replenish the ranks. At any rate, it's nice to see you so interested in old friends like Jarel. I hope you'll extend me the same honor."

Tamara laughed good-naturedly. I watched enthralled. Once she'd finished, she asked, "What do you think Jupiter meant when he said Cupid is the most powerful god of all?"

"It's a mystery to me," I answered. "But I do so love a good mystery."

Tamara studied my eyes a moment, perhaps searching for a flicker of falsity. She would find none. Satisfied, she advanced to her next question, which she leaned in to whisper. "How long exactly could you hear Cupid's thoughts?" She pulled back quickly enough to catch my sheepish grin. I stopped dancing. She led me for a mere moment to keep us moving. "You couldn't hide that secret very well, Bacchus."

"I could hear him since the night before I met you," I answered truthfully. She stilled, and it was my turn to keep us waltzing. What I wouldn't have given to hear *her* thoughts at that moment. I looked over to see Cupid glaring at me, his eyes drilling into mine. I shifted my attention back to his flame. "Before you ask, yes, he thinks only of you."

Tamara kept her face unreadable until she further inquired, "Can you still hear his thoughts?"

"No. That ended tonight." I leaned in. "Do the others know my secret?"

"I don't think so," she said.

"I will write a great play about our adventure," I promised. "Even those already here will wish to learn what happened before they were players."

Tamara raised a doubtful brow.

I assured her, "For all it does, theatre allows us to press our noses against the window. I promise they'll want to see in. And I will dedicate the play to you, my dear."

Tamara shook her head. "Oh, I don't think Cupid will like that."

I openly smirked. "Never fear, my sweet. He'll never know." I twirled Tamara under my arm before bringing her back to me. At her questioning look, I added,

"Cupid is averse to reading, judging by the piles of scrolls in his castle with unbroken seals. Vulcan won't read, either, as he spends his free time tinkering, and we should all thank the gods for that. You certainly can't read my play to check its veracity."

"And why would you say that?" she asked with the tiniest hint of offense. "I can read."

"Of course you can. Obviously. And I'm sure you do it well, but people should never believe that which is written about them lest it affect their fate. And you, Tamara, you respect Fate more than most anyone here."

Tamara nodded, and I could tell she was not one to let curiosity get the better of her. All the better to romanticize my tale.

Cupid tapped my shoulder at just that moment, about to rob me of my final moments with his princess.

"What about *Fate*?" Cupid asked. The eavesdropper.

"I was complimenting Tamara on her ability to work out The Fates' riddles," I replied.

"You do nothing *but* compliment her," Cupid said through closed teeth.

"A compliment is something like a kiss through a veil," I said. "Victor Hugo."

Cupid resorted to gritting his teeth.

My, how I'd miss this teasing!

Cupid turned to his beloved and conceded, "I still don't know what I was supposed to contrast."

"Vulcan's crown," Tamara answered breezily, as if it were the simplest thing in the world. "The Fates said, 'Contrast love, no start, no end.' The crown, a ring, has no start or end, unlike love, which has a definite start when you meet that special person and can certainly end if you were wrong about it. 'Contrast hearts, its goal to mend.' The crown is meant to mend hearts and minds, whereas love, well, love can break either."

"Not *my* love," Cupid said, and took Tamara's hand for the waltz. He stepped ever so slightly in front of me. "You've had your turn, Bacchy. I'm cutting in."

It wasn't the most polite of intrusions, but I suppose if another guy were dancing with my girl, I'd want to cut in, too. I would have to find another dance partner tonight, as I always do.

I looked around. The merbrigade swayed in the waters tinged pink by the Opera House. Jupiter's guests twirled happily while stepping into whatever food my cats and the royals' pets weren't eating. I noticed my panthers eyeing the fowl once more. I pursed my lips, repeating my unspoken warning. We have an understanding, you see. I allow almost anything, as do they, but we both have our boundaries, and we mutually respect them.

I noticed that the love angel with the sleek black wings (Tyrone, I believe, Cupid's former chauffeur) had danced several rounds with the same angelette, a short, big-bottomed girl. When I looked back at Tamara, she was pointing it out to Cupid. I guessed that was soon to be settled as well.

I took a step forward and was immediately doused in wine. Pip materialized before me.

"I'm so sorry, Mr. Bacchus," Pip flustered. "I've got to get used to these extra wings. My speed is a bit out of control. But I brought you the decoy crown and a glass of wine in thanks."

"In thanks for what?" I asked.

"For everything," he replied.

I slapped Pip on the back. I'd been too hasty in judging him.

"Let's share a drink, Pip," I offered.

Wine conquers all.

(Crew, thus ends the tale. Dim the lights slightly as The Fates were right. Merrymaking and good cheer were to be found in this belvedere. Be sure to keep the light slightly stronger on Juno. She is on her third glass of wine. She's ahead of me. Let the record show...)

Bacchus – Roman god of theatre, wine, and merrymaking. Instigator. Bestower of ill-devised wishes. Son of Jupiter. Contender for Tamara's hand.

Jupiter – God of the sky and thunder, king of the gods, husband (and brother) of Juno, and brother of Neptune. Prodigious philanderer. Father of Mars and grandfather of Cupid (though neither by blood).

Neptune – God of the seas and earthquakes. Hard sleeper. Brother of Jupiter, uncle of Cupid, and father of Triton and his many subordinates in the merbrigade.

Mercury – God of commerce, journeys, boundaries, trickery, thievery, and communication. Conducts dreams and guides the newly deceased to The Underworld. Jupiter's son and lead royal messenger. Malcontent.

Cupid – God of love, affection, and desire. Son of Venus and Mars, grandson of Jupiter (though not by blood). Recently dethroned for sloppiness but reinstated through determined grit.

Triton – The sea's messenger god, famed for generating giant waves by a blow on his conch shell. Son of Neptune and leader of the merbrigade.

Cyclopes – One-eyed giants fathered by Neptune. Their single eye, situated in the middle of their forehead, likely takes up much of their brain space, for they aren't very bright. What the poor creatures lack in acuity, however, they make up in aggression. Do not make the mistake of encountering a hungry one.

Pantira – Bacchus' troupe of black panthers. The three fierce felines pull his chariot and serve as his guardians and helpers.

Tamara – Cupid's leading lady. Daring adventurer and astute decipherer. Previously one of the famed Fallen Four and one of even fewer beings who've trespassed in The Underworld and lived to tell the tale.

Cerberus – Tamara's three-headed hellhound, Cupid's bestest dog friend ever, and the former guardian of the entrance to The Underworld. Current guard of Cupid Castle, its inhabitants, and its resident koi fish.

Morta – One of the three Fates, those goddesses of destiny who speak in riddles, measure lifespans, and guard Heaven's Gate. They are older and likely stronger than the reigning monarchs. Morta's terrifying scissors sever a mortal's thread of life, making her the most feared of the trio.

Pip – Cherubic celestial messenger. Was instrumental in Cupid's recent and infamous dethronement. Talkative but colorful.

Vulcan – God of volcanoes, lava, fire, and metalworking. Son of Jupiter and Juno. Captor of the latter. Husband (and constant pursuer) of Venus. Tinkerer. Inventor. Genius.

Merbrigade – Defending force of the seas. Comprised of merfolk from all waters of the globe. Under the command of Neptune and his royal line.

Venus – Goddess of love, beauty, and fertility. Married to Vulcan yet is a frequent paramour of Vulcan's brother, Mars, with whom she bore Cupid. Rumored to have advised Cupid during his dethronement (further rumored to having been ignored, much to his detriment).

Mars – God of war, father of Cupid, and the most prominent "other man" in Venus' life. Brother of Vulcan and thus constantly in his crosshairs and often in his snares.

Quadriga Horses – Mars' massive, fire-breathing black stallions, trained in war and marshaled four abreast to pull his chariot while intimidating all in sight.

Three little girls – The Fates disguised. Those goddesses of destiny, measurers of lifespans, and guardians of Heaven's Gate often speak in riddles, nudging fate their way. Nona spins the thread of life, Decima measures its lifespan, and Morta ends lives in the thread's cutting.

Roosters – Mercury's pets, mascots, and lookouts. They crow the day and its news just as he crows his royal messages.

Celestials – All those immortals who reside in or are a part of the divine kingdom of Olympus.

Habandash – Jupiter's personal assistant charged with overseeing Olympic and Earthly affairs. Deposed Cupid and instated a fraud in his place. Later reestablished Cupid as Olympus' lead lover.

Eagle – Jupiter's pet and protector, a constant companion and helper to his master.

Juno – Goddess of the state and marriage, queen of the gods, and sister/wife of Jupiter. Mother of Mars (via sheer will) and grandmother of Cupid. Detector and punisher of Jupiter's mistresses. Disgruntled anniversary ball "honoree."

Tyrone – Love angel and former chauffeur, personal assistant, and spy to Cupid.

Jarel – Apprentice to Mars, former butler to Cupid, previously the Fallen Angel who introduced Cupid to the remaining members of The Fallen Four (he, Tamara, Tommy, and Cornelius).

Tommy – Assistant to Habandash, in charge of providing The Still Fallen plentiful opportunities to regain Heaven's Goodwill. Previously one of The Fallen Four and Tamara's most devout defender.

Cornelius – Assistant to Habandash, in charge of adding the names of those to be lovified to The Hit List, previously one of The Fallen Four.

Dragon – Vulcan's hitherto unseen creation, weapon, and pet. Its lava body is now known to be covered in bronze and gold plates, surely removable by Vulcan alone. Attempting to remove said plates is most unwise.

Acknowledgments

There are certain people who've been so instrumental in the creation of this book that I feel their names belong in the byline right along with mine. I cannot thank them enough for their insight, encouragement, and stick-to-itiveness.

Chief among these hardy souls is my husband, Jeff Miracola, who sees life as one big action scene with lots of dragons and goblins throughout. He's also absurdly optimistic, which is a good trait for a creative soul and yet another reason why I'm glad he's around.

I thank Valerie Biel, Keith Pitsch, and Christine Esser, for going line by drudgy line through the first, second, etc. renditions of the original manuscript and making them better each go around. These three fabulous people form the best writers' group ever, and I am deeply indebted.

I thank my kids for cheering me on, especially Antonia, whose great ideas ended up on these pages. Thanks, Honey.

And finally I thank the Roman gods themselves for providing such fertile creative ground. They consume my thoughts and often make me chuckle to myself as I imagine their reactions to modern quandaries, thus making me the crazy lady laughing at nothing. Once again, thanks gods. Thanks a lot.

Silvia Acevedo is a television personality and former news anchor who's spent many years reporting objective fact. She's interviewed presidential candidates, covered national and international stories, and given breaking news reports for CNN and local television and radio stations around the country. She also occasionally guest hosts a morning talk show for a local NBC affiliate. Roman gods, however, were shockingly absent during this time, so Silvia decided to put fiction – especially mythology – back into her life.

In *God Awful Thief*, Silvia deftly weaves vignettes of ancient myth with a wholly new and laugh-out-loud story for the modern age. The stage is set for a wild adventure in this rousing encore to the first act in the *God Awful* Series of Books.

Silvia lives with her husband, Jeff Miracola, who is an accomplished fantasy illustrator and children's book artist, and their children just outside of Milwaukee.

Find her at www.silviaacevedo.com.

Word of mouth is crucial for any author to succeed. If you enjoyed this book, please tell your friends and leave a review on your favorite website.

We at Three Points Publishing are grateful for your support.

THREE POINTS
PUBLISHING

Read the adventure that started it all!

God Awful Loser
by S. Acevedo

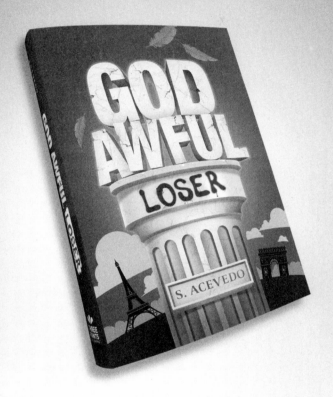

➤ And ➤

Cupid's exploits continue in Book Three of the *God Awful* Series of Books.

Soaring your way in 2017

WWW.THREEPOINTSPUBLISHING.COM